Evelyn

Evelyn James has always been fascinated by history and the work of writers such as Agatha Christie. She began writing the Clara Fitzgerald series one hot summer, when a friend challenged her to write her own historical murder mystery. Clara Fitzgerald has gone on to feature in over thirteen novels, with many more in the pipeline. Evelyn enjoys conjuring up new plots, dastardly villains and horrible crimes to keep her readers entertained and plans on doing so for as long as possible.

Other Books in
The Clara Fitzgerald Series

Memories of the Dead

Flight of Fancy

Murder in Mink

Carnival of Criminals

Mistletoe and Murder

The Poison Pen

Grave Suspicions of Murder

The Woman Died Thrice

Murder and Mascara

The Green Jade Dragon

The Monster at the Window

Murder Aboard Mary Jane

The Missing Wife

Grave Suspicions of Murder

by

Evelyn James

A Clara Fitzgerald Mystery
Book 7

Red Raven Publications
2018

Chapter One

The newspaper report on the sad death of Mr Isaac Graves stated that he had passed peacefully at his office desk one dull April morning. It made a great deal about his work with local charities, his regular support for Church fundraisers and the time he devoted to the committee that tended to the Brighton Pavilion. It mentioned his still living mother, (now in her eighties and a keen lady golfer) and his sisters, before reporting that his widow had asked for donations to a good cause rather than flowers at the funeral. Mr Graves had disliked flowers due to his acute sinus problems.

At no point did the newspaper so much as hint that Mr Graves' death had been anything more than a sudden fluke of fate. There was not a whiff of the possibility of it being anything other than natural. Which was why Clara Fitzgerald, Brighton's first female private detective, was startled to receive a visit from Mr Graves' former business partner, Mr Erikson, to ask her to investigate his late associate's death.

According to Erikson there was every reason to fear that Mr Graves had died from that deadly disease called murder, and he was quick to point a finger at several suspects.

The problem was that Clara could not see any real proof for the suggestion. Mr Graves had not been in the best of health, considering he was only just into his fifties. He had had a bad bout of pneumonia over the winter which had left him weak, and the stress of his job as a solicitor tended to damage his health further. He took on too much work and spent too much time at his office. He didn't eat well, nor did he get enough sleep. He compensated by smoking a pipe continuously and constantly sucking mint imperials that he kept in a paper bag on his desk. Most people had not been very surprised when his death was announced. He was the sort of person you expected to die sooner rather than later.

But Mr Erikson was adamant that there was more to the matter and Clara took on the case more to stop him causing any trouble for the grieving family by spreading his suspicions abroad, than from any real conviction that she would find anything. It was better, she concluded, that she investigate the case thoroughly and provide Mr Erikson with proof that his suspicions were unfounded, than to let the matter rumble on secretly and for rumours to tarnish Mr Graves' memory.

The morning of the funeral was as grey as the day poor Mr Graves had died. The newspaper had painted a detailed picture of the dedicated solicitor found slumped at his desk, still working through the paperwork of a particularly tricky will. There had been an outpouring of grief in the town, for quite a number of people knew Mr Graves either through his work, or through the charitable causes he supported. There was expected to be quite a turn out to the funeral, and there had been a private announcement that a horse-drawn hearse would take Mr Graves from his home and, if people wished to pay their respects, they could do so by lining the streets along its route. Needless to say this rather informal suggestion had attracted quite an audience, some of whom were more curious gawkers than real acquaintances of the deceased. Though there was a nice turn out from the Ladies' House of Reform, (which Mr Graves donated his money and time to regularly) with a long line of women in black stationing themselves along the road as a mark of respect.

The hearse was the finest Mr Clark the undertaker had in his yard. Pulled by a magnificent ebony stallion, with black feathers on his head and a real strut to his elegant trot. The horse was blinkered to avoid him being distracted by the crowd and normally Mr Clark would have expected the whole procession to go quite smoothly. The black stallion was, after all, hugely reliable, and had never been a bother. He knew the right pace to walk so that the mourners behind could keep up without having to endure the indignity of walking briskly or (heaven forbid!) having to run. In fact, Mr Clark had no inkling that morning that his funeral procession was about to become the talk of the town for all the wrong reasons.

Clara had positioned herself at the corner of the road just before the church to pay her respects. Like many in the town she had a vague knowledge of Mr Graves, though she had not made more than a passing acquaintance with him. She had recently been encouraged (some might term it press-ganged) into joining the Royal Pavilion Committee of Friends, which endeavoured to keep the building looking spic and span, and open to the public when convenient. Mrs Wilton, a former client, had persuaded her to join with the remarkable insight that it would be good for Clara's business to be seen serving the public. Clara thought this a little far-fetched, but somehow she had allowed herself to be persuaded. So far she had only attended a single meeting and had been briefly introduced to Mr Graves when someone pointed him out across the table. They had nodded at one another. Clara had not taken much notice of him at the time. He was an ordinary, middle-aged man, who looked very tired, but spoke with great enthusiasm. Had she known he was about to die in odd circumstances she would have paid greater heed.

Clara stepped to the very edge of the kerb and peered

around the line of people next to her to glimpse the hearse travelling up the road. Mr Clark looked very formal in his top hat and black suit and there was quite a row of mourners walking behind the hearse, at the head being the grieving widow who was heavily veiled and impossible to recognise as Mrs Grace Graves. Clara was just thinking that, if nothing else, Mr Graves was going to get a good send-off, when Mr Clark's reliable black stallion suddenly reared up and bolted. The poor undertaker was cast to the floor as the horse started to charge. There was panic from the mourners as the dearly deceased started to hurtle down the road and who knows where he might have ended up had not a couple of lads from the gathered crowd had the instinct to jump out and grab the stallion's reins.

Mr Clark came running up, completely flustered by the ordeal. He had never experienced such an episode in all his many years of ferrying the dead back and forth. As he went to take the reins of the agitated horse his top hat blew off and over the back of the stallion, before landing on the road by the hearse's wheels. Clara stepped off the pavement and picked it up, brushing a speck of dust off the brim. The mourners were catching up. They were looking most indignant at the scene, well, at least those not wearing veils were. It was difficult to say what the heavily concealed widow was thinking.

Mr Clark was thanking the lads who had stopped the runaway horse and trying to get proceedings back underway as fast as possible. He reached over the back of the stallion to take his hat from Clara, and it was as she handed it over that something spooked the horse once more. With a terrible neigh of outrage, the horse bolted yet again and Clara could not move out of the way in time. There was an awful moment of pain as the hearse ran over her right foot and she collapsed backwards onto the pavement with a cry.

For a moment Clara hardly dared move. Her foot felt on fire and, casting a cautious glimpse at it, she half expected to see it mangled out of all shape. There was a little bit of blood and the foot was swelling and going red as she looked at it, but she had been lucky in that the hearse wheel had slipped over the middle of her foot quite quickly and the damage was not as severe as it might have been.

Someone was calling for a doctor. As it happened there was one on the opposite side of the street. He came running over to assess the situation. He gently removed Clara's shoe, though she had to grit her teeth to keep from crying out again. The damage was more visible with her shoe off. The mark of the wheel was plain to see, but her toes had been untouched and the doctor was optimistic when he saw the damage that the foot would heal with rest.

Rest? Clara was appalled. She had a case to attend to and rest was the last thing she was able to do. But she had to admit she was not going to be walking anywhere anytime soon. The slightest movement of her foot was agony.

Mr Clark was mortified at what had just occurred. He rushed to Clara and made profuse apologies. Never had his horse bolted like this, never. He would have to have the vet out to see if he was ill, and he would pay for Clara's medical bills, naturally. Clara waved him away. It was an accident and, though it hurt dreadfully, she was not going to blame Mr Clark for it.

The two lads who had stopped the bolting horse the first time now came to Clara's aid. Between them they carefully lifted her up and stood either side of her, while she rested her good foot on the ground and gingerly held up the crushed one. The doctor insisted on accompanying her home. It seemed a long walk. Even moving carefully Clara felt every step in her damaged foot and by the time she reached home she was about fit to burst into tears and sob over her misfortune.

Annie, the Fitzgeralds' maid and loyal friend, opened the door and stared at Clara's unhappy face.

"What on earth have you done? You only went to a funeral."

Clara suddenly felt embarrassed.

"I was run over by the hearse," she admitted.

Annie stared at the scene for another second or two, then she began to giggle.

"Oh Clara, only you could be run over by a hearse!"

Clara did not see the humour in the situation as she was carried into the parlour and deposited in her favourite armchair. The doctor set about bandaging her foot, while Annie went to make tea. Clara looked at her foot miserably.

"How long will it take to heal?" she asked.

"You will need to give it a few weeks at least," the doctor said. "Maybe a couple of months."

Clara felt even worse.

Annie returned with a tray of cake for Clara's helpers and a hearty piece for Clara herself. The doctor declined staying for a cup of tea as he had a funeral to attend. But the lads who had carried Clara hung around for some time, explaining how the horse had bolted and how Clara had been run over.

"Never knew old Bill to act like that," one shook his head. "Bill, being the name of the horse, naturally."

"Is he the black stallion Mr Clark always uses for special funerals?" Annie asked.

"That he is."

"He pulled the hearse for the late mayor," Annie nodded. "I thought he looked a sound creature."

"He pulled my parents' hearse," Clara added.

There was an uneasy silence as the spectre of death seemed to have crept over the tea party. The lads finished their cake and made their excuses. Clara thanked them for their help as they left. Then she flopped back into her chair and let the full misery of the situation take over her.

"Oh, Clara, it won't be so long," Annie saw her face and tried to make amends for laughing earlier.

"I have a case to investigate," Clara said miserably.

"It will have to wait."

"It can't."

Annie pressed her lips together, trying to think of a solution. At that moment the front door clattered again.

"That will be Tommy home," Annie said, with a touch of relief. "He went with Oliver to visit Herbert Phinn."

Tommy, Clara's older brother, appeared in the doorway. Tommy had been confined to a wheelchair since the war. If anyone should have sympathy for Clara's current condition, you would imagine it should be Tommy.

"Hey ho, there she is! The woman who can't resist trying to catch speeding hearses with her foot," Tommy was grinning and it was clear there was going to be little sympathy for Clara's plight.

"The news is all over Brighton of what happened," Oliver Bankes, the Fitzgeralds' friend and Brighton's police photographer, winked at Clara. "You won't live this one down in a hurry."

"You are both horrid," Clara groaned, looking at her poor foot. "It hurt a lot!"

"Ah, now, we didn't mean it," Tommy changed his tone. "Is it very bad?"

"The doctor says I must rest, and how am I to investigate my case like this?" Clara pointed at her foot.

For a moment no one spoke, then Oliver piped up.

"You need a detective by proxy," he said. "Someone to do all the footwork, excuse the pun, for you. You can still piece all the evidence together once they bring it back."

"And precisely who do you have in mind?" Clara asked forlornly.

Again no one spoke, then, first Tommy, then Oliver, looked at Annie. Annie didn't notice at once, but when she did she jumped up like a startled rabbit.

"Oh no!"

"You could do it Annie!" Tommy declared. "Who else can Clara trust? Besides, it would be awful for her reputation if she handed over responsibility to a man, think what people would say."

"But I would have to visit people!" Annie looked aghast.

"You could do that, old girl, you have helped out before."

"Helped," Annie clarified. "Not acted as a detective!"

"Supposing you did do it, Annie," Clara was looking at her keenly now, "you would get me out of a bind, and it would only be for a short time. You would be my eyes and ears."

"Really!" Annie shook her head.

"What else can I do?" Clara pleaded. "If I back out of this case, it will just be awful. Will people want to hire me afterwards?"

"You can't help being hurt," Annie insisted.

"But people don't think like that. They just get cross because I didn't handle their case," Clara fixed her eyes on Annie. "Annie, this time I really need your help."

Annie felt hemmed in. She had only one argument left.

"What about the housework?"

"We can arrange something," Tommy brushed the difficulty aside. "Perhaps hire a temporary maid?"

"I think not!" Annie snapped.

"Well, we will work something out. You won't be rushing around like Clara does, just doing odd errands."

Annie looked back at Clara, who did her best to look persuasive.

"I really need your help," she said.

Annie knew she was beaten. She took another look at Clara's bandaged foot and sighed.

"Fine then, I shall be a detective by proxy, but don't expect me to do anything dangerous."

"When do I do anything dangerous?" Clara declared.

They all gave her a stern look.

Chapter Two

Clara's foot was propped up on a stool. She glared at the broken appendage as if it had done something wrong.

"It won't get better any faster with you casting the evil eye on it," Annie said as she pinned her hat to her head. "Do I look respectable enough to visit a solicitor?"

Annie was masking her emotions well, but she was very nervous about her first day as a detective.

"You always look respectable, Annie," Clara assured her. "Probably more so than I do."

"Well, I just hope Mr Erikson is understanding about my replacing yourself in this case."

"He really has to be understanding, I can't do anything else," Clara frowned. "Remind him that I will be going over all the evidence you gather personally, so he doesn't think I have completely abandoned the matter."

"Do you think poor Mr Graves was done in?"

"I am open minded on the subject, as I must be on any case. And, avoid using phrases like that around Mr Erikson, he may not take them well."

Annie pulled on her coat.

"Now, I have left the potatoes on the table in a bowl for you to peel. Tommy is in charge of the bacon joint. I gave him all the instructions for it."

"I assure you, we shall have dinner ready for when you return."

Annie looked less than convinced.

"I've got a jam roly poly ready to boil. But I should be home in time to do that," Annie gave Clara one last look. "And don't sit here all morning feeling sorry for yourself. I told Tommy to fetch some books from the library for you when he went with Oliver. Oh, and Dr Cutt is due to visit at half two to check your foot."

Clara nodded, wishing she was the one now leaving the house. She had already had enough of being an invalid.

"I'll be off then," Annie picked up her handbag and took a deep breath.

"You will be fine," Clara promised.

Annie glanced back.

"I will try not to let you down," she said over her shoulder as she headed out.

Mr Erikson and Mr Graves had a nice suite of offices in one of the older properties in town. It boasted their names above the door and in the front window was a discreet advertisement for their various services. Mr Graves was noted as a specialist in wills and the various legal matters that could result from a sudden death. Annie paused to wonder who would be dealing with the tricky matter of Mr Graves' unexpected exit from this life? Would it be Mr Erikson? Or would he be considered a little biased in the matter?

Oh dear, Annie mused to herself, I am beginning to sound like Clara already!

Annie opened the door of the solicitor's building and found herself in a neatly appointed reception area. A well-dressed middle-aged woman sat behind a high wooden desk and peered at Annie through half-moon glasses.

"Good morning," the woman said briskly.

"Good morning," Annie tried her best to still her grumbling nerves and pretend she had Clara's confidence. "I have an appointment to see Mr Erikson."

The receptionist glanced down at a book before her. "Miss Fitzgerald?"

"I am her representative, Miss Green. She called ahead to inform you of the change."

The receptionist ran a finger along the entry in her book.

"Ah, yes. I shall see you up," the receptionist stood and escorted Annie through a doorway and up a set of stairs. They found themselves on the first floor, heading towards a door marked 'Mr Erikson'. The walls were lined with oil paintings of historic battles, which Annie assumed were meant to be metaphorical for the legal battles the solicitors dealt with every day. Though she rather found them unsettling.

At Mr Erikson's door the receptionist asked her to wait, then tapped lightly on the wood. A voice summoned her to enter and she disappeared for a moment to announce Annie's arrival. When she reappeared she informed Annie she could enter, before returning to her desk downstairs.

Annie found Mr Erikson sitting at his desk. He was a stern looking man with sharp features and a very beaky nose. He seemed to hunch in his suit like an old scarecrow in a field and his appearance did not make Annie feel precisely welcome.

"Miss Green?" he asked.

"Yes," Annie approached the desk, feeling a cold sweat coming over her. "Clara, I mean, Miss Fitzgerald, 'phoned concerning the change of plans."

"She did, do please take a seat. I was sorry to hear of Miss Fitzgerald's accident. How is she doing?"

"More annoyed about being unable to leave the house than anything else," Annie shrugged. "She is rather a rotten patient."

Mr Erikson laughed at this candid remark and suddenly he did not seem so intimidating. The suit seemed to sit better on his shoulders and his stern look almost vanished. Annie relaxed a little.

"So, you are acting as her agent?" Erikson asked when his amusement subsided.

"Yes, but she said I must assure you that she will be looking at all the evidence I gather personally."

"Of that I have no doubt, I have heard good things about Miss Fitzgerald's thoroughness and efficiency. It was why I went to her in the first place. Tell me, did you know Mr Graves at all?"

"I did, just a little," Annie answered. "He went to the same church as my parents, and used to help out at all the fundraisers and fetes."

"That sounds like my colleague," Mr Erikson gave a long sigh. "I met Isaac when he was just finishing his legal training. I was a few years older than him and established in my father's firm, but I wanted to branch out. I persuaded Isaac to join me in my business venture. I put in most of the money, but he repaid me well over the years. He spent countless hours in these offices dealing with case after case. I felt almost lazy in comparison. He was dedicated to his work and to his clients. Mr Graves cared, that is why people came to him."

"But then why would anyone want him dead?" Annie said bluntly before she could stop herself. She could have kicked herself. She had done exactly what Clara had warned her not to do.

"Oh, all solicitors, however diligent and fair, find themselves confronted with the occasional aggrieved client. I dare say Isaac had his fair share, though we rarely exchanged views on our cases, so I cannot say with any degree of certainty what those grievances might have been. Then there was always his family."

"His family?"

"Yes. Isaac had an elderly mother he cared for, and several sisters, all unmarried. His mother and sisters reside in a rather splendid red brick Victorian manor house, just outside Brighton. Isaac paid all their bills. There was some money left over in investments from his late father, but not enough to keep the widow and the daughters in the style to which they were accustomed. I am aware that Isaac's generosity towards his mother and sisters did not always sit well with his wife, Grace."

"She did not appreciate all his money going to them?"

"I think it was more a case that she did not like the long hours he worked just so he could provide for both his own, and his mother's, household. I think she felt his family took liberties over his income."

Annie nodded, an understandable complaint from a wife who must have felt a tad neglected.

"But none of that amounts to a desire to kill poor Mr Graves, surely?"

"I see you are thinking of motive, and I concur that nothing I have stated equates to a good motive for murder. Unless, of course, Isaac had finally had enough of one or other of the parties he was tied to."

"Hardly his wife."

"No, but, supposing he told one of his sisters that he was no longer going to pay all their expenses? They might imagine they would be better off with him dead and their share of any inheritance he left, than to be 'cut off'."

Even Annie could see that statement required a hefty amount of speculation.

"I take it from your look you think I am being irrational. Perhaps I ought to offer some proof for my case, after all, I am a legal man, and I know these matters cannot be dealt with on hearsay alone," Erikson opened a drawer and produced a sheaf of papers. "I am the executor of Isaac's will. When I was studying its contents shortly after his death I was alarmed by some of the details. In fact, that was the reason I went to Miss Fitzgerald in the first place. What I expected to find in Isaac's will was an even distribution of his assets. Instead, I discovered that one of his sisters was to get the lion share of his estate, while his remaining family, including his wife, were due only token amounts. It struck me as a very odd will for any responsible man like Isaac to make."

"How do you explain it?"

"I cannot, except that for some reason Isaac felt the need to favour one of his sisters out of all proportion to the rest. Even more curiously, this will was made in the last few months. Shortly after his bout of pneumonia. His prior will I had seen and I knew its contents well enough. It was a very clear distribution of his money evenly between the family. Completely different from the will I found among his important papers."

"Could the will be fraudulent?"

"That would not be unheard of, but I found it in our private safe. As far as I am aware, I am the only other person to know the combination for the safe. Though, I could be mistaken on that," Erikson sighed. "So much for motive, now let me explain what first troubled me about Isaac's death. I was the one who found him, you know."

"Oh dear, I am sorry," Annie said sympathetically.

"Yes. We always dined together at midday. It was my little insistence; else Isaac would continue to work without eating anything. We always went across the road to the pub and had sandwiches and a pint of beer each. Isaac never kept good track of time, so I would fetch him a few minutes before midday. It was a routine we had lived by for years," Erikson paused for a moment, as his memories caught up with him. "That dreadful day I walked along the corridor to his office and knocked on the door. No one responded, which was strange because I have an arrangement with our receptionist to book no appointments for Isaac after eleven. We all looked out for him, you see.

"I knocked again, but still no reply, and I started to feel uneasy. Isaac was forgetful over time, but he never ignored someone at his door. There had only been one other time when he had not responded to my knock, and that was when he had been taken bad with pneumonia in his office. He never should have come into work that day, mind you, but he did. Isaac was dedicated like that. On that occasion, when he had not answered his door, I had mulled over the matter, left it for a while, then returned and tried again. When I still received no response I opened the door and he was slumped at his desk, hardly breathing.

"So, you see, when all this happened in just the same manner a second time, I became extremely worried. I hammered on his door and then opened it. There he was slumped at his desk yet again. I imagined a relapse and ran to Miss Parker downstairs to ask her to call for a doctor. It was only when the doctor arrived that we discovered he was dead.

"The obvious assumption was that he had suffered heart failure from his weakened condition, but something seemed odd to me. For a start, the doctor said he had been dead for at least an hour, or thereabouts, but I could have sworn I heard someone leaving his office just half an hour before I went to knock. I remember thinking that Isaac had been with his ten o'clock client a long time. Of course, I could be wrong about what I heard. But then I noticed the glass on his desk. There was a glass of water, almost empty. Isaac never had a drink on his desk, in case it should spill and ruin the document he was working on. Equally, I had never seen him drink a glass of water. Tea, yes. Beer, yes. But Isaac was not a man who drank water. The glass and pitcher were reserved for the use of clients and, even then, they were not allowed to be placed on his desk."

Mr Erikson paused and spread his hands out palm up, as if to say 'that is all I can offer you'. Annie felt it was rather loose evidence to start speculating on a murder over.

"What was Mr Graves working on when he died?"

"The only document on his desk was a will for one of our clients. She has just passed and there is some concern among the family that the will is not correct. I assume Isaac was studying the details, trying to discover if their concerns were founded, when he died. The client liked to change her will often, and in situations like that there is always argument over whether the final will is the correct one. I advise clients to store their wills with us, then there can be no argument as we will only keep the last legal version they created. But some clients insist on keeping their wills at home. I do believe Isaac's client had the disagreeable habit of keeping several previous versions of her will, as well. We advise against that, naturally, but you can hardly go into a person's house and check for out-of-date wills, can you?"

Annie felt they were going off topic. Unless Mr Erikson had suspicions about Isaac's final case?

"No, no," he answered when she posed the question. "I do not suspect anything of the sort. Besides, Isaac was only just starting on the problem. It would have been pointless killing him at that stage, I would imagine."

"Who was the last person to visit Isaac?" Annie asked, feeling that, despite their lengthy conversation, she had no real concrete proof to bring back to Clara that Mr Graves had been murdered.

"Mrs Hatton. I can give you her address. Unfortunately, I do not know what the meeting was about."

"A will, perhaps? Mr Graves was a specialist in that area," Annie suggested.

"Perhaps, but I really could not say."

By the time Annie left the solicitors' office and set off for home, she felt she had few insights to offer Clara. Mr Erikson's concerns were based on very little indeed, except for a possible door slamming. She wondered what Clara would suggest? Perhaps digging deeper into the matter? Well, at least her first interview had passed without incident, that made Annie feel better. She stopped at a flower shop to buy a bunch of daffodils, then headed for home.

Chapter Three

Dr Cutt peered over his ancient pair of spectacles. He contended that he only needed them for close work and had not bothered to have his eyes checked in years. As a result he was wearing glasses far too weak to be of any assistance to his vision. He almost had his nose pressed to Clara's foot as he studied her bruises.

"You were very lucky, young lady," Dr Cutt finally stood up and went to his bag for more bandages. "The damage is relatively minor."

"So I shall be able to get up and walk about soon?" Clara asked hopefully.

"Oh dear me, no," Dr Cutt shook his head. "The foot is a delicate instrument. It needs time to heal sufficiently. I suggest at least two months of complete rest. I would not even expect you to attempt to put on a shoe with a foot in that state."

Clara glowered at her foot moodily.

Tommy rolled himself into the room at that point.

"Clara, how do you tell if bacon is burning? It smells odd… oh, Dr Cutt," Tommy looked sheepish at the sight of the doctor. "I thought you had finished."

"No, my boy, bandages to be put on as yet. But I am glad to see you," Dr Cutt was grinning like a spider who has just caught a fly. "I was growing concerned when you missed our last two appointments."

"Tommy?" Clara gave him a stern look.

Tommy had the decency to look abashed.

"So much was going on," Tommy deflected the comment. "I just forgot about the appointments."

"Ah, good, because I was concerned you had decided against my treatment suggestion," Dr Cutt smiled, he was in his eighties and a true man of medicine who could not imagine retiring. He was also a very progressive doctor, who had spent a great deal of time studying the causes and symptoms of shell-shock. Dr Cutt was firmly convinced that Tommy's inability to walk was due to a mental trauma, rather than physical damage. Tommy had certainly suffered plenty of both while serving in the trenches, but his problems with his legs still remained a mystery to himself and those around him.

"What treatment had you suggested?" Clara interjected.

It had taken a good deal of persuasion to get Tommy to see Dr Cutt in the first place. She had not known Tommy was skipping appointments with the doctor.

"I was thinking that hypnosis might prove therapeutic. You have heard of that?"

"I recall it was quite popular in the last century for helping hysterics," Clara said, regretting her words when Tommy glared at her.

"I am not a hysteric!"

"No, of course not," Dr Cutt smoothed over the error. "Hypnosis has far more wide ranging uses than just treating hysteria. It helps to tap into the unconscious mind, as I said to you before, the problem you have with your legs is due to a mental block, and if we can break it, then you shall walk again."

Tommy still looked uncomfortable. He was always ill-at-ease when people started talking about the vagaries of the mind, especially his mind. He was not convinced by all this psychology lark and it deeply troubled him that he was somehow stopping his legs from working because of a problem in his head, not in the physical muscles. Tommy was very much a man of his age, and he believed mental illness was something that only occurred to the weak willed. He had no ill-will towards those that suffered from such complaints, but he found it deeply troubling to imagine he was one of them.

"Surely it is worth a try, Tommy," Clara said very gently. "Imagine if hypnosis helped you to walk again?"

"We have experimented with the use of sedatives," Dr Cutt added, "with some success, but I need to use more direct methods to reach the unconscious mind. It is perfectly safe, I might add, I have been performing hypnosis for the last forty years."

Tommy looked unconvinced.

"How does it work?" Clara asked.

"I begin by asking the patient to focus on an object, say my pocket watch, then I gently put them into a state of deep relaxation, as if they were asleep. Only, I can still communicate with them, and ask them to do things. However, they will never do anything out of their nature, or that would harm themselves. After extensive study it has been proven hypnosis cannot make a man walk off a bridge, say, because even in an unconscious state the body is acutely aware of self-preservation. Nor could you ask a man under hypnosis to do anything against his own moral code. I could not make Tommy murder someone, for instance."

"Then, I see no harm in trying it," Clara fixed her eyes on her brother. "If it works, then you will walk again, and wouldn't that be utterly wonderful? And if it doesn't, then nothing is lost."

Tommy knew they were talking sense, but still hesitated. His attention wandered to his legs. Why could he not use them? Why did they not obey his commands? Doctor after doctor had told him that nothing was physically wrong with his legs, yet, no matter how hard he tried, they refused to move.

"Perhaps I could offer a demonstration?" Dr Cutt suggested, "Miss Fitzgerald, might you be willing to try first?"

"I suppose I would," Clara said. "But I have nothing you can cure by hypnosis, unless you can fix this foot of mine."

"No, no, it will be a pure demonstration of the process," Dr Cutt stood before her. "Now, if I might ask you to look at my watch, good. Focus on the watch face. Feel all your body relaxing, your limbs feel light as a feather. You are feeling very tired, going to sleep would be good, yes? Let your eyes shut, good, good. You are very calm. Your body is floating on a cloud of air. Nothing matters, nothing hurts. You are deep, deep asleep."

Dr Cutt paused and looked at Tommy. Carefully he picked up one of Clara's hands, then let it go so it flopped back down onto the arm of her chair. She appeared completely relaxed and unaware of him.

"Now, Miss Fitzgerald, might I ask you to repeat the entire list of the kings and queens of England from 1066, as you learned in school?"

"Clara could never remember all those," Tommy interrupted politely, but before he had finished speaking Clara had begun reciting a list of names. As he listened in amazement, she rolled off the complete lineage of the monarchy from William the Conqueror without a single mistake.

"The unconscious mind remembers everything," Dr Cutt explained. "There is nothing hidden to it."

Clara finished the recital and fell silent.

"Thank you, Miss Fitzgerald, now, I want you to awaken. You are rising back up from slumber, you feel the chair beneath you again, you can hear the clock ticking. That's it, wake up and open your eyes."

Clara awoke and blinked. She glanced around the room as if things might have changed in her absence, but all was the same.

"You did very well, my dear," Dr Cutt patted her hand.

"Turns out all those history lessons weren't wasted on you after all," Tommy added.

Clara looked at him baffled.

"Now, Mr Fitzgerald, are you convinced?"

The smile fell from Tommy's face.

"Reciting a list of kings and queens is very different from getting a man walk again," he said.

"Not to the unconscious mind," Dr Cutt corrected. "It is all about pure memory. We just need to remind your waking mind how to walk again. Will you not at least try?"

Tommy grimaced, but then he saw the look on Clara's face. She wanted him so desperately to try, and she had even made herself a willing guinea pig to prove that hypnosis was safe. He found he was feeling guilty about his reticence. At the worst, it could just fail. Though that in itself filled Tommy with dread. He didn't have much hope left that he would walk again, but what little he did have was incredibly fragile. He was scared of trying hypnosis in case it didn't work and he was left with no hope at all. But, he supposed, that was a sort of cowardice as well, and Tommy had never considered himself a coward.

"Very well," he said at last. "Do your worst, doctor."

"I would much rather do my best," Dr Cutt said good-humouredly.

He took out his pocket watch and repeated the procedure he had just demonstrated on Clara. Tommy took longer to go under. He was agitated and resistant. But when he did go, he went very deep. Dr Cutt moved back a little and observed his patient.

"Now Tommy, we are going to get you to stretch those legs," he said. "Let us begin by raising the right leg up from the knee."

Clara was astonished to see Tommy raise his leg and extend it straight out. She stared in pure amazement.

"Very good, now put that leg down and try the other

one."

Tommy repeated the action with similar ease.

"Excellent, now, I shall offer you my arm and you will very slowly rise from your wheelchair, do you understand?"

Tommy gave a nod. When Dr Cutt walked to him and offered his arm Tommy took it and, with a degree of difficulty, for his muscles had wasted, he slowly stood. He was leaning quite heavily on Dr Cutt, but the old physician did not seem to notice.

"Now, let us see if we can take a few paces forward," Dr Cutt instructed.

Patient and doctor walked across the rug for about three paces, then Tommy wobbled a little.

"You are doing very good, but your legs are tired. We need to build up your strength. Let us go back to the chair and sit down."

They returned to the wheelchair and Tommy lowered himself stiffly down.

"Now Tommy, I have a very specific thought for you to remember. I want you to remember that your legs do work, you have just demonstrated that, and when you awake you will be able to lift your legs up from the knee as we did first off. Now, I want you to awaken slowly. You are rising from slumber. You can feel the chair you are sitting in. You can hear the clock ticking..."

Clara watched as Tommy was gradually roused from his deep slumber. Like her before him, he blinked rapidly and glanced around as if he expected the room to have changed while he was under hypnosis. Then he looked at Dr Cutt.

"Well?"

"Ask your sister, dear boy," Dr Cutt smiled.

Tommy turned to Clara, looking confused.

"You walked Tommy!" Clara declared excitedly. "I saw it!"

"My legs ache," Tommy said, completely baffled. "They ache."

"That is because you walked!" Clara insisted.

"Now, we have much work to do as yet," Dr Cutt interjected. "We need to strengthen your legs before we can progress further. For the next week I want you to practice lifting your leg from the knee and stretching the muscles three times a day, for about ten minutes."

"But, doctor, I can't lift my legs!" Tommy protested.

"Are you implying I don't know my own patient?" Dr Cutt asked with a knowing smile on his lips. "At least try, dear boy."

Tommy looked at him aghast, then at Clara. They both seemed to have lost their minds in the brief time he had been unconscious.

"Try," the doctor insisted.

Tommy pulled a face, knowing he would fail at the request. Grumpily he lifted his leg in the manner he had attempted to do on so many occasions without success. He was immensely surprised when his muscles obeyed him for the first time in three years. He stared at his right leg which was now straight out before him. Still amazed he put it down and lifted his left leg. It obeyed too!

Tommy was incredulous.

"What did you do?" he asked the doctor.

"Only what I said I would. I tapped into your unconscious thoughts and planted a new idea there."

Tommy shook his head as if this was a dream and any second he would find he had been mistaken.

"Now do you believe me?" Dr Cutt grinned. "Well, my dears, I must be going. I have another house call to make. I shall return this time next week, if that is suitable, and we shall deal with your foot Miss Fitzgerald and we will work again with your legs, Mr Fitzgerald."

Tommy was too astonished to speak.

"That would be lovely doctor," Clara told Dr Cutt, feeling almost as excited as her brother by the developments.

Dr Cutt said his goodbyes and said he would let himself out. Tommy was still too dazed to think straight.

"Did I really walk?" he asked Clara.

She nodded.

"Only a few paces, your legs need to be strengthened. But you most assuredly walked."

Tommy didn't know what to say. He was still sitting in confused silence when Annie arrived home. She appeared in the parlour and glanced at them.

"You are both oddly quiet," she said suspiciously.

"It has been an odd sort of afternoon," Tommy answered.

"Dr Cutt has had Tommy walking, Annie!" Clara could not resist spreading the good news.

Annie suddenly brightened.

"Is it possible?"

"Show her what you can do," Clara instructed her brother.

A little embarrassed at being the centre of attention, Tommy nervously lifted first his right leg and then his left. Annie was so excited she clapped her hands.

"Oh Tommy!" she ran to him and kissed his cheek. "Are you not thrilled?"

"I'm just a bit… disbelieving at the moment," Tommy smiled. "It doesn't seem real."

"But it is real," Clara said firmly. "Now, if only Dr Cutt could use his powers to heal my foot faster…"

"Oh, you are always so impatient!" Annie tutted with amusement at Clara. "Anyhow, I have some information for you, though I doubt you will find it interesting. Mr Erikson has very little to base his suspicions on."

"I feared as much," Clara sighed.

"I think he mainly feels…" Annie paused and sniffed the air. "Is that my bacon joint burning? Oh, Thomas Fitzgerald!"

Annie darted out of the parlour to rescue dinner. Tommy rolled his eyes.

"You see how much more important bacon is to her than my legs?"

Clara chuckled.

"I am sure she will forgive you," suddenly she frowned as a thought crossed her mind. "Wasn't I supposed to have peeled the potatoes?"

Chapter Four

Annie was not looking forward to her next assignment from Clara. Mr Erikson's conviction that he had heard a door shutting could not be ignored. It might be nothing, or it might be a clue. Clara was still not convinced there was any crime to investigate, but she had to gather evidence, even if it was only evidence that demonstrated Mr Graves had died of natural causes. As a man of the law Erikson would only be consoled by hard facts, and Clara needed to find them.

So she had sent Annie on an errand to track down Mrs Hatton, the last person (probably) to see Mr Isaac Graves alive. Mr Erikson had been kind enough to offer Annie the lady's address, even though it was a slight breach of client confidentiality. He negotiated around this by concluding that, as she was not his client, he was not precisely breaching her confidentiality if he just happened to know where she lived and passed this information on to an acquaintance.

What really worried Annie was the fact that Mrs Hatton lived in Old Steine, one of the grander parts of Brighton, and the place where the 'old money set' resided. Mrs Hatton was a relative new comer to the crescent shaped close, her husband having bought the property when they were first married. He was something to do with politics and had inherited a lot of money from his own father, who was a Victorian coal magnate. Annie was very nervous about speaking to such an upper class person, who would surely see through her facade at once and recognise a maid trying to play at detective?

But Clara was insistent that Mrs Hatton must be interviewed, and would go out the door herself if necessary. Annie had put her foot down on that idea; Clara was staying put and resting. Besides, Annie was going to do a light dinner with the left over (mildly charred) bacon, and there were plenty more potatoes to peel. Extracting a promise that Clara would not forget her kitchen duties this time, Annie had ventured out the door in her best hat and coat, hoping Mrs Hatton was a reasonable person.

She had no appointment for the visit. Clara had endeavoured to arrange one without success. The Hattons had a 'phone, but no one answered when Clara rang. There was a possibility they had left the town for the season, but Clara hoped that was not the case. Otherwise she would have to attempt to extract information from Mrs Hatton by letter and that was never a productive affair.

Annie was, therefore, hopeful that no one would answer when she rang the bell of the large house, with its Georgian portico and impressive bay windows. She was disappointed when a maid appeared.

"Is Mrs Hatton in?"

"She is just home, but I can't say if she is receiving visitors," the maid said.

"Could you ask her if she would be prepared to talk to me about the late Mr Graves? It is a matter of tying up loose ends for the family. My name is Annie Green. I am working on behalf of Clara Fitzgerald."

The maid took this all in without curiosity and then went to find her mistress. She was a long time and Annie began to wonder if she would be sent away. It was becoming rather awkward to stand on the steps with people wandering past and wondering who she was. There was a man selling milk across the road and he was watching her with unabashed interest. Annie pretended she hadn't noticed.

At last the maid returned.

"Mrs Hatton says she don't know any Clara Fitzgerald."

"I didn't expect her to," Annie replied. "Please can you explain that we are working on behalf of Mr Erikson, I really only need a quick word to confirm a few details."

Annie suddenly had a notion of how to grab the woman's attention.

"There has been some slight confusion over the matter of a document Mr Graves was working on," she added.

The maid disappeared once more and Annie waited impatiently. How did Clara do this day in and day out? Did she not become infuriated with people? The maid was not gone so long this time. When she reappeared it was with good news.

"Mrs Hatton says she can give you a few moments before she goes out to lunch. Please come this way."

Annie followed the maid inside, feeling a little awestruck by the grand staircase before her and the large oil paintings on the wall. There was a crystal chandelier hanging from the middle of the ceiling and Annie found herself wondering how on earth someone cleaned such a thing. She hoped the Hattons had more than one maid.

Mrs Hatton was waiting in the morning room. It was nearly eleven o'clock but she was still surrounded by the debris of breakfast time. Dirty plates and cups sat on a table to one side, making Annie itch to pick them up and wash them. A newspaper had been discarded on a chair and Mrs Hatton herself was lounging on a sofa in her dressing gown. She was smoking and looked in no rush to get to her lunch engagement.

Annie assessed the woman. She was in her forties, but trying to pretend she was still in her twenties. Her hair was unnaturally dark for her eyebrows, which suggested she dyed it. She had the remains of make-up (presumably from the previous day) on her face and she looked tired. There were shadows beneath her eyes suggesting she had had a lot of late nights recently, and far too many early mornings. She gave Annie a languid look.

"What is this about a document?"

"There is some confusion at Mr Erikson's office as to precisely what business Mr Graves was engaged to do on your behalf. He died, you see, before leaving any directions. You were his last client that day, I believe?"

Mrs Hatton gave a shrug and drew on her cigarette.

"I imagine so. I had an appointment at half ten with the dear man."

"And it was for a will?"

"No, actually..." Mrs Hatton paused. "Who precisely are you?"

"Miss Annie Green, working on behalf of Miss Clara Fitzgerald," Annie was armed with a selection of Clara's business cards and she now handed one over. "Miss Fitzgerald was unfortunately injured at Mr Graves' funeral and can't personally investigate. So I have come on her behalf."

"A private detective?" Mrs Hatton dropped the card on a side table. "Why would Mr Erikson be asking you to do his work?"

"There is an awful lot to arrange with Mr Graves' sudden death," Annie lied smoothly, feeling more like Clara with every moment. "We are merely providing a helping hand. You can rely on our complete confidentiality."

Mrs Hatton smoked her cigarette and there was a long pause before she spoke;

"If I was to ring Mr Erikson's office, would he confirm what you are doing?"

"Yes," Annie said, not entirely sure that was true.

Mrs Hatton stubbed out her cigarette.

"Would you please sit? I feel most uncomfortable

when people stand over me."

Annie took a chair opposite the woman. She sat on the edge, still rather nervous.

"Mr Graves was arranging a few private legal matters for me. Did he leave any paperwork on his desk, when he...?"

"He was slumped over his papers," Annie replied.

"Then surely Mr Erikson must know what he was working on?"

"But he doesn't," on that Annie was certain. "He thought it might be a will, because Mr Graves was a specialist."

Mrs Hatton was starting to look very worried, her lips were pulled down into an exaggerated grimace of unhappiness, like the Greek masks sometimes stitched onto theatre curtains. Annie realised that she had discovered something important, at least, she was pretty certain this was important.

"Are you suggesting, Mrs Hatton, that some papers important to yourself might have gone missing?"

"They should have been on the desk, we were merely finalising details," Mrs Hatton shook her head. "But you say Mr Erikson knows nothing of the matter? And he must have been through everything..."

Mrs Hatton reached out for her cigarette case and found it empty.

"Damn!"

"Should I ring the maid to bring more?" Annie offered, not quite out of the habit of serving others.

"No need, I have some on the mantelpiece," Mrs Hatton stood, the effort seeming to weary her. She went to the mantel and took a handful of cigarettes from a box, before returning to her seat. She wasted several moments refilling her cigarette case, then lit one and started to smoke again.

"I am deeply concerned that those papers are missing," she said as the cigarette burned down between her fingers. "And I can't understand how this might have happened.

"There is one small matter that may account for it," Annie said gently. "We are investigating the possibility that someone slipped into Mr Graves' office without an appointment."

"Who?"

"We can't say. It is just that Mr Erikson believes he heard someone leaving Mr Graves' office not long before midday."

"I was gone by a quarter to eleven at the latest," Mrs Hatton looked anxious. "Are you suggesting someone went in and stole my papers?"

"Not precisely. Until I came here, we were not aware that any papers were missing."

"You have to find them. It is extremely important. Perhaps they have just been misplaced?"

"What was in these papers?"

Mrs Hatton gave a groan.

"They were the legal arrangements for divorce proceedings," she sighed. "Mr Graves had just finished preparing them and I had gone to the office to confirm the details. The next step was to deliver them to my husband, but then Mr Graves died and I have not had a chance to consider what to do next. I supposed Mr Erikson would want to see me. I thought that was why you were here."

"I'm sorry," Annie said. "I will inform Mr Erikson at once and hopefully he can find the papers. They may have been confused for something else."

They both knew that was extremely unlikely to be the case.

"May I ask how Mr Graves seemed when you last saw him?" Annie changed the topic.

"Seemed?" Mrs Hatton was puzzled by the question. "He was his usual self. Talkative, friendly, professional."

"He did not seem ill?"

"No," Mrs Hatton looked sad. "I was quite astonished to hear of his death. I knew he had been unwell over the winter, and perhaps he was not quite as strong as he once was, but I never expected him to die."

"I think it was unexpected for everyone."

"I know his wife," Mrs Hatton confided. "I honestly thought the shock of his death would destroy her too. She goes to the same bowls club as me. She was devoted to her husband, though he was a man driven by his work. She could hardly get him out of the office. Did you know, they had not been on a holiday in twenty years. Mrs Graves confided that to me. Not even for a weekend. He even worked through the Bank Holidays. She was lucky to keep him at home on Christmas Day. I suppose, in truth, it was a difficult marriage. Lopsided, if you see my meaning."

"I think I do," Annie agreed.

"Unlike my marriage," Mrs Hatton gave an odd snort. "I would be quite happy if I knew my husband spent all his time at his office and not elsewhere. But such is life."

They were silent a moment, then Annie remembered something Clara had reminded her to ask.

"Did you have a glass of water while in Mr Graves' office?"

"No, I was only there, what? Ten? Fifteen minutes?" Mrs Hatton shook her head. "There was no need."

"Was there a glass of water on Mr Graves' desk?"

"What an odd question," Mrs Hatton's forehead wrinkled in confusion. "I really can't remember. I suppose I looked at the desk as we were making the final arrangements. I signed my name to the papers after all. But a glass of water? I don't recall one, but I wasn't really paying attention."

"I don't suppose you saw anyone coming in as you were leaving?"

"No. Look, if these papers have gone missing," Mrs Hatton refrained from using the word 'stolen', "then what is Mr Erikson going to do about it?"

"I cannot answer for him," Annie said honestly.

"If they fell into the wrong hands..." Mrs Hatton wrung her own hands together. "My husband has enemies. He is an important man. It comes with the territory."

Annie felt helpless to assist the woman. All she could do was report back the loss and hope Mr Erikson knew where the papers were. It did, however, add a new dimension to the possibility that someone had stolen into the office between eleven and midday. Not that that meant Mr Graves had been murdered, but perhaps someone had seen an opportunity?

"I will inform Mr Erikson at once," Annie promised. "Now, I have already taken up too much of your time."

"Oh, don't think on it," Mrs Hatton waved a hand to dismiss the comment. "I was bored anyway."

Annie saw herself out, leaving behind a very worried Mrs Hatton. She felt sorry for the woman, even if she did seem a little insipid. She walked back beneath that monstrous chandelier and the maid met her at the door.

"Thank you," Annie said as the door was opened for her, feeling decidedly odd that she was the one being waited on for a change.

She wandered into the street and considered what she must do before heading home. She would need to see Mr Erikson and let him know there may have been a theft from his office. What an awful thought! Who would do such a thing? Well, someone who wanted to blackmail a person she supposed. It was starting to look as though Erikson's ears were not playing tricks on him after all.

It was only when Annie was halfway down the road and mulling over what she had in the pantry to go with the bacon for dinner, that it occurred to her that she only had Mrs Hatton's word for the time she had left the office. She could be lying. But what would be the purpose? And all this fuss about divorce papers – would she be making that up if they had not really disappeared? Annie decided she was confusing herself unnecessarily. The woman had seemed honest enough and lying about getting a divorce was a dangerous matter should it leak back to her husband. No, that was not a lie, though she could still have been in the office longer than she stated. But Annie had the feeling that Mrs Hatton was a dead end, other than possibly being another victim in this strange saga. It suddenly seemed that there was a lot more to Mr Graves' death than met the eye.

Chapter Five

Clara had placed a large piece of paper before her, upon which she intended to create a chart of clues and evidence in the Graves' case. So far there was not a lot on it. Aside from a misplaced glass of water and some missing papers, (which may or may not have simply been misfiled in the confusion after Mr Graves' sudden death) all she had was Mr Erikson's assertion that he had heard a door opening and closing long after Mrs Hatton had left the building. But that hardly amounted to murder. In fact, it hardly amounted to anything. Clara tapped her pencil lightly on the paper. Where to look next? Who to ask? So far she had yet to prove to herself that there had been foul play, let alone any hint of a suspect.

Annie placed a cup of beef tea on the table. She was utterly convinced that beef tea could cure all manner of ailments, including broken feet.

"It doesn't look promising," she said, looking down on the piece of paper.

"No. What is your take on all this Annie? What was your feeling when you talked to Mr Erikson?"

Annie shrugged her shoulders.

"I don't know."

"A large part of detective work is about instinct.

Having a feeling for something. Maybe something that seemed minor at first, but that would bear fruit if examined further?" Clara tried to tease out something from her friend. She had overlooked explaining how useful it was to analyse a witness' manner of speech and general demeanour when she sent out Annie. It was something she hardly noticed herself doing in the first place, but now she realised how important such observations could be.

Annie mulled for a while.

"Mr Erikson did not seem terribly impressed by any of the Graves family. I think he felt they rather used Mr Graves."

"The mother and his sisters, you mean?"

"Perhaps also the wife. Or maybe he felt she was a little hard done by."

"Realistically, if Mr Graves was murdered, the first suspects would be his close kin. Someone who perhaps knew about the change in his will. But, then again, they were rather late to kill him after the new will had been created."

"Unless the will was fraudulent?" Annie suggested. "Then perhaps someone would wish him dead before the fraud could be discovered?"

"The sister who received the bulk, for instance?" Clara considered this, "We need to know more about the family. Which is why I have invited Mrs Grace Graves around for tea. I suggested she might help me to go over some business her husband had left incomplete with the Brighton Pavilion Committee. Also, we must arrange for Tommy's friend, Herbert Phinn, to take a look at Mr Graves' final will."

As she spoke the clock on the mantel chimed a quarter to four. Clara carefully folded up her piece of paper and asked Annie to place it in a drawer. They had not long finished when the doorbell rang. Annie went to answer it and showed in Mrs Graves.

The widow was a little younger than her husband, but

had not worn quite so well. She looked drawn and as if she had lost a fair amount of weight rather too swiftly. There were unpleasant sags of skin beneath her chin, as if she were a toy someone had pulled the stuffing out of. She was dressed all in black, but had dispensed with a veil. Her dress was quite modern, a straight low-waisted number that masked a great deal of her weight-loss. She looked very unhappy; grey shadows gave her eyes a bruised look and she stared at the floor rather than meet Clara's eyes. She did not look a merry widow, but rather a woman who greatly begrudged her loss.

Clara asked her to sit and apologised for her own inability to move.

"I saw what happened," Mrs Graves said as she took a seat, perching right on the edge of the chair as if she might need to spring up at once. "I was just behind the hearse. I do apologise."

"Hardly your fault," Clara said kindly. "Accidents occur."

"My husband would have been mortified to think his own hearse ran you over. And when you were fetching the undertaker's hat too. Mr Clark was very distressed over it and has insisted on offering us a discount on any future funerals."

"How kind," Clara said, finding the idea morbidly humorous. "May I ask how you are Mrs Graves?"

"I…" Mrs Graves stared into the fireplace, then she gave a little sigh. "I don't know how to describe the way I feel. Just… just I am so very tired and so sad. I miss my husband. The house seems empty, which is strange considering he spent so little time at home. But there was always the anticipation of him coming home, if you see what I mean. Now I have nothing."

"It is never easy to lose someone dear," Clara said, the comment rather innocuous, but Mrs Graves didn't seem to mind.

"I suppose I shall find a way to compensate. My mother is still alive and has asked me to live with her.

Perhaps I shall. I don't have any children, so there is really no need for me to stay in that big house."

Clara politely overlooked the financial considerations of the move which Mr Graves' unusual will would have caused.

"You had some business to ask me about?" Mrs Graves added, making an effort to change the subject.

"It's a very minor matter, but, as you know, I joined the committee for Brighton Pavilion recently and Mr Graves was our Chairman."

"Yes."

"At our last meeting it was arranged that a local builder would be contracted to deal with the leaky roof. As Chairman, Mr Graves was to sign the agreement when it was drawn up to give his approval. With his sudden… Now that he has left us, we have agreed that for all contracts and agreements arranged before he went, we should ask you to act as his proxy. It is really only a formality. The papers require his signature, or that of his agent, as he was named in them."

Mrs Graves seemed to be only half listening. She gave a nod.

"Isaac loved the Pavilion," she murmured.

Clara passed her the papers. It was fortunate she had been placed in charge of them at the last meeting, just before Mr Graves' untimely demise. They gave her the excuse she needed to assess Mrs Graves without rousing suspicion.

"Would you care to join the committee, Mrs Graves? In memory of your husband?"

Mrs Graves shook her head.

"No, that was his affair."

"I have no doubt this is a trying time for all the Graves family. How is Mr Graves' mother taking it?"

"Who can say? She is made of sterner stuff than to be left devastated by the loss of her only son," there was a hint of bitterness in Mrs Graves' tone, but she masked it well.

"I believe I saw her in the funeral cortege, heavily veiled and followed by her daughters."

"Yes. She is still quite spry considering her age and health. They say she has a bad heart, but it does not seem to stop her."

"She will miss her son though?"

"She will miss his money," Mrs Graves laughed sourly. "He worked all the hours God sent to please her and ensure she could live in the manner she was accustomed to. He drove himself into the grave for her and his sisters."

"I am sorry to hear that."

"I was not completely surprised when I heard he had passed at the office. Though, I thought it would be a heart attack."

"Was it not?" Clara asked curiously.

"No. At least, the coroner who examined my husband said there were no overt signs of his heart giving out," Mrs Graves pursed her lips. "There were no real signs of anything, except that he had died. His throat was a little swollen, that was all. He had not been strong after his attack of pneumonia."

"That is a withering disease," Clara agreed.

"He wore himself down, Miss Fitzgerald. Our doctor told him time and again that he must take better care of himself. Plenty of sleep, regular meals, but would he listen? We all tried our best for him, I know Mr Erikson was very good at making sure he had something at lunchtime. But the man worked himself into the ground. I suppose in many ways I expected this."

"He was a dedicated solicitor."

"He was a dedicated son and brother," Mrs Graves gave a bitter laugh. "He killed himself to make sure his sisters had good dresses and meat on the table seven days a week. That his mother might still have a carriage and footman, even if she barely used them. He kept them in feathered hats and silks, and what did they do in return? Complain, that was all. They never had enough and my husband was such a good man that he wore himself down trying to please them."

Mrs Graves gave a slight moan of sorrow. She pressed a black handkerchief to her mouth.

"I tried to make life simpler for him. I tried not to ask for much. All I wanted was for him to come home at regular hours and eat dinner with me. But I could never compete with the demands of his family."

"I'm sorry," Clara said gently.

Mrs Graves did not seem to be listening anymore.

"May I say," Clara added as a silence opened before them. "Mr Graves was very fortunate to have a wife so understanding as yourself."

"Understanding?" Mrs Graves almost laughed. "Oh, I wish that were so! I put pressure on him too, just not financial pressure. I was always asking him to come home early, or to spend the weekend with me. Do you know we had not been away on holiday in over twenty years? Not since his father died, in fact. He said he could not afford the time. I so wanted to have a week in Cornwall with him, just walking and breathing the sea air. I was certain it would do him good. I suppose I was just too late."

"It sounds as if Mr Graves was his own worst enemy."

"That he was. But I shall miss him deeply. Was there anything more you wanted?"

Clara said there wasn't. Mrs Graves made her excuses and departed. Clara felt she had gained very little from the interview, other than proving even more conclusively that Mr Graves was a prime candidate for death from exhaustion. Still, there was more evidence to examine.

Clara headed for the 'phone in the hallway and looked up the number for the Brighton Constabulary. Then she made a call to Inspector Park-Coombs.

"Inspector, how do I get hold of Dr Deàth?"

Deàth was the only coroner in Brighton and it seemed most likely he had been the one to attend to Mr Graves. The Inspector promised to pass a message along that Clara wanted to speak with him. There was no telephone in the morgue, but Dr Deàth had one in his office. A short time later Clara's 'phone rang and the friendly voice of Dr Deàth answered her when she said 'hello'.

"Miss Fitzgerald, how may I help you?"

"Good evening, Doctor, have I called you away from anything important?"

"No, no. I was just finishing up here before heading home. The wife has a bridge party organised. Do you play bridge? I can't stand it myself, and everyone gets very agitated when I mention my work. People are surprisingly squeamish about what is a very natural process. Death must come to us all."

"Indeed," Clara had never known a man so content with his work and with his own mortality as the coroner. "I wondered if you could help me?"

"Has someone died?"

"Not anyone I know, at least, not recently. Actually I wanted to ask you about the unfortunate demise of Mr Graves the solicitor."

"Oh that. Yes, very tragic."

"I have been asked to investigate some unusual circumstances concerning the death," Clara explained. "Needless to say, this is all confidential."

"Absolutely," Deàth assured her, his ears now firmly pricked.

"What was the cause of Mr Graves' death?"

"I shall be completely honest with you, Miss Fitzgerald. Mr Graves' death was one of those that seemed to have very little cause. He was in a weakened condition after his bout of pneumonia. I found a number of lesions on the lungs that indicated he may have had trouble breathing. The heart, however, seemed healthy, and there were no obvious signs of a particular disease. There was some swelling in the throat, which may have been due to a number of reasons, none of which were particularly suspicious. My best conclusion was that he had simply stopped breathing. Sometimes it happens."

"Could the swollen throat have been a sign of

something sinister?"

"Asphyxia?" Deàth was silent for a moment as he considered the possibility. "Had there been marks on the neck I might have considered it. He was a man who had trouble breathing, therefore it would only require relatively minor pressure to cause him extreme difficulties. Had he been in his bed, we might have wondered about a pillow across the face. If we were suspicious of the death, naturally. Smothering could be possible, but I saw no evidence for it on the scene."

"What of poison?"

"That is a wider spectrum for speculation," Deàth confirmed. "A number of poisons can affect the breathing. Equally, for a man in such a condition of ill health as Mr Graves was, some usually harmless substances might have proved hazardous. Smoke, for instance, might have caused his throat to swell as his body overreacted to the stimulation. I once had a case where a man died from being caught in a thick smog. He was an asthmatic and the smog brought on an attack. Clara, does someone believe Mr Graves' death was unnatural?"

"There has been some speculation from a certain party, yes. But I can find no evidence to back the suspicion."

"There was nothing on the body to indicate violence," Deàth mused. "I don't like the thought of being wrong."

"At this stage, I very much doubt you are," Clara assured him. "But I want to temper these speculations before they cause any harm."

"Indeed. Well, if I can be of any further help, do call."

Clara thanked Dr Deàth and put the 'phone down. As she retrieved her paper from the drawer she mulled over the matter yet again. Mrs Graves had given her no indication that someone would want her husband dead, in fact his mother and sisters were better off while he was alive. And Dr Deàth was good at his job and would have spotted something amiss. Really, the evidence was mounting up against Mr Erikson's suspicions. Perhaps, for once, Clara was to discover an innocent death rather than a murder. Clara tapped her pencil on the paper again. So why was it the more she dug into the matter, and the more she found evidence against murder, the more she began to have her own suspicions about Mr Graves' tragic end?

Chapter Six

Annie had a busy morning ahead of her. Her first port of call was the home of Mrs Graves, Isaac's mother, and her daughters. Clara had given her the covering excuse of paying her respects on the bereaved family. As Clara's agent, Annie was entitled to pay a call and offer condolences. Equally, Clara had intended to offer a donation to a good cause the ladies favoured instead of buying flowers for the funeral. However, her accident had belayed this desire, and now she was sending Annie to make amends. Of course, she also had the distinct ulterior motive of seeing if there was any clue the ladies could offer about Mr Graves' sudden death. After all, there was still the mystery of the new will.

Mrs Graves and her daughters lived in a double-bay red house, set in mature gardens. The path to the house was laid with gravel and crunched under Annie's feet. She was nervous again. Meeting Mr Erikson was one thing, being confronted by the Graves family was far more daunting. She tried to distract herself by naming the shrubs in the border as she went past and wondering how old the gnarled wisteria was that grew over the front door. It did little to help. When she reached the door she reminded herself that she was here on quite legitimate business, before ringing the bell.

The door was opened by a woman in her late forties. She stared at Annie through a pair of small spectacles.

"Yes?"

"I have come on behalf of Miss Clara Fitzgerald to pay her respects and to offer her apologies for being unable to attend the funeral of Mr Graves."

"Well, she was run over by my brother's hearse," the woman was suddenly amused. "I think she can be forgiven."

"She also wished to give a donation to a worthy cause of your choosing, as she was not able to do so at the funeral."

"You best come in then," the woman seemed a lot less formidable. "I thought for a moment you were another of those awful press people who keep calling."

"Press people?" Annie asked in confusion.

"Yes. We have had dozens of them on the doorstep. Someone has suggested to them that my brother may have died under suspicious circumstances."

The stunned look on Annie's face was completely genuine, though not for the reasons the Miss Graves before her might imagine.

"Who would say such a thing?" she was thinking about Mr Erikson. Could it be he had let his suspicions slip?

"There are always those who see the worst in perfectly innocent situations," Miss Graves shrugged. "I am Annabel, by the way, I shall introduce you to the rest. We are very informal. It saves time, don't you think?"

She escorted Annie to a well-appointed sitting room where the sharp April sunlight was pouring in on four women. Three were around Annabel's age, the fourth was a great deal older and was clearly Mr Graves' mother.

"Here we have my sisters Agatha, Christiana and Julia. And this is my mother. Now, what was your name?" Annabel turned to Annie.

"Annie Green."

"Right ladies, this is Annie Green who has come on behalf of Miss Clara Fitzgerald who, apparently, is feeling rather bad that she missed the funeral."

"Nonsense!" declared Mrs Graves, "She was run over by the hearse, wasn't she?"

"Yes," Annie answered. "But she was unable to offer her donation instead of flowers because of the incident, and wanted to make amends."

"Really, what a fuss," Mrs Graves snorted. She was a tall and lean creature, who looked surprisingly sturdy considering her age. Robust was a fine word for her. She looked likely to live many years as yet. "Is Miss Fitzgerald recuperating well?"

"She is, though she is very impatient to be on her feet again," Annie found she was actually warming to the Graves women. They were not so intimidating and clearly did not take much heed of common pretensions.

Annabel offered her a chair and fetched a cup of tea. There was an open box of fudge on the table, and she asked Annie if she would like a piece. Annie declined. Fudge she found too sweet and sickly.

"I do feel poor Isaac would be mortified to think he ran over one of his own mourners," Julia Graves said, helping herself to fudge. She appeared the youngest of the sisters, with fair blonde hair that draped about her shoulders.

"A rogue horse is hardly Isaac's fault," Annabel chimed in. "Isn't Miss Fitzgerald on the Brighton Pavilion committee?"

"Yes," Annie said. "That was how she knew Mr Graves. She was shocked, as we all were, by his sudden passing."

"It was unexpected," sighed Mrs Graves. "And after he had recovered so well from the pneumonia. I fear he returned to work too soon."

"He detested being stuck at home," Agatha Graves added. "I don't mean to speak ill of Grace, but my brother found home-life tedious. He lived for his work. I can't imagine he enjoyed being trapped at home all those weeks he was recuperating."

"Mr Erikson was good enough to send some papers to his house for him to work on in bed," Mrs Graves took up the thread of the story. "I know Grace was cross about it, but really he was going stark mad lying in bed with nothing to do. A man like Isaac cannot survive on the limited stimulation of newspapers and novels for days on end. He needed something to get his teeth into."

"He was a specialist in wills, I believe?" Annie said.

"Yes, he was good at intricate wills that would trouble other people," Mrs Graves smiled proudly as she thought of her son. "As he would explain it, most wills are simple things, but sometimes people have such complicated financial arrangements in life, that they require a similarly complicated arrangement in death. He was very good at untangling such matters and making sure monies were directed to where they ought to go. I remember he worked on the will for that tinned meat fellow, what was his name Annabel?"

"Mr Matthews. He had founded a company on tinning pork and beef. Most households have such a product somewhere in their larders."

"Yes, that's him. Well, Isaac had endless dramas over his will because he insisted on constantly adding codicils, you know, the little additions you can put at the end of wills. One minute he was disinheriting his sons, the next he was leaving the estate to them. It went on for years! Isaac handled the legal side of the will when Mr Matthews died. It proved quite complicated to unravel all the alterations he had insisted on making during his lifetime.

"The silly man did not understand that making a new will would have solved a lot of problems, just kept altering the original," Mrs Graves tutted. "But that was the sort of work Isaac relished."

"He will be sorely missed," Julia Graves spoke softly. Of all the family she seemed the quietest and the most distressed by her brother's death. She had grown pale during the conversation and now looked almost sick to her stomach. Annie wished she could try to comfort her in her distress.

"We will all miss him," Mrs Graves concluded. "Life will not be the same without his visits."

"And this matter of the newspaper folk is so inconvenient," Agatha added. "Really, who spreads rumours of murder?"

Julia swallowed hard as if she was about to be sick. Annie found herself wondering precisely which sister had been given the lion's share of Isaac's estate. It was not a question she could ask the family and she had failed to get the information from Mr Erikson. Julia was the sister who looked most distressed. Was that meaningful?

"I say, Miss Fitzgerald is a detective!" Annabel perked up. "Perhaps we should ask her to dig into this matter? Find who has been spreading this nonsense! Put an end to it."

Annie shifted uncomfortably in her seat.

"Miss Fitzgerald is rather incapacitated," Mrs Graves reminded her daughter. "Besides, I am certain this matter will blow over soon enough."

"I can't see how anyone could imagine Mr Graves had been murdered," Annie interjected, feeling she should offer something to the conversation. Clara would be most aggrieved if she did not follow up this train of thought when she had the opportunity.

"Some people see suspicion everywhere," Annabel said stoutly. "It all began just a few days after his death was announced, if you recall mother? That man from the Gazette appeared on the doorstep and wanted to know if we had heard the rumours. I sent him packing with a flea in his ear."

"People always speculate over sudden deaths," Agatha shrugged. "But we shouldn't bore Miss Green with that nonsense."

Annie wanted to say she was far from bored, but it would be deeply suspicious to do so. Instead she found the interview coming to an end. She arranged for a donation to be sent to the Children's Hospital, the cause the Graves family had chosen to receive the money people would normally have spent on flowers.

"I did wonder why there were no flowers at the funeral," Annie said as she handed over a cheque Clara had prepared for her.

"Isaac was allergic to a great deal of things," Mrs Graves explained. "Flowers gave him awful hayfever. After his bout of pneumonia he was even more susceptible. He detested them. A single whiff of roses would have him sneezing for a week."

"It would have been rather ironic to put flowers on his coffin," Annabel voiced the unspoken thought everyone else was thinking. She was the bluff sister who tended to speak in a forthright manner.

At the door Annie tried to find a way of bringing up the possibility of Mr Graves being murdered again, but she could not find the words. Frustrated, she said goodbye and headed off down the path. She had the shopping to do and needed to pay a visit to Mr Erikson to ask for the will so Clara could examine it. She was feeling no further forward.

She was just opening the garden gate when she was accosted by a man standing half hidden by a bush that grew over the wall.

"Hey, miss?"

Annie glanced up in surprise. She took in the man's appearance; shabby coat, dusty shoes, rain damaged hat, and suspected he was a tramp.

"I have no money on me," she lied quickly.

"I don't want your pennies. I want to know why you were visiting the Graves family?"

Annie took another good look and noticed that he had a pad of paper and a pencil in his hand. Ah, so he was a newspaperman.

"I was merely paying condolences on behalf of my employer," Annie answered, trying to move around the man.

He blocked her way.

"Who is your employer?" he asked.

Annie glared at him and tried to step past. He blocked her again. Annie grumbled to herself.

"I work for Miss Clara Fitzgerald."

"Ah, Brighton's premier private detective? And what is her interest in the Graves?"

"Nothing more than mutual sympathy. Clara… I mean Miss Fitzgerald, worked on the Pavilion Committee with Mr Graves."

"So she is not investigating the possibility he was murdered?"

Annie snorted with derision.

"What is all this nonsense of murder about? Why should anyone murder Mr Graves?"

"Ah, well that is the question. But I have it on good authority that his death was not altogether natural and that someone benefited significantly from his death."

"Then you should go to the police."

"Without proof?" the reporter laughed. "All I have is speculation. But it does make you wonder. A man goes to work and dies at his desk. I have seen the coroner's report, I have my sources, and there is no evidence to suggest what killed him. The more you look at it, the more you have to ask yourself, was it natural?"

"You are lacking a motive," Annie pointed out, finding herself inclined to argue with this annoying man.

"I'll admit that is a sticking point. Mr Graves does not seem to have had any enemies. Though I do find myself wondering about his associations with the Ladies' House of Reform."

"I hope you don't intend to disturb the family with all this nonsense," Annie moved past him at last. "They hardly need such speculation on top of their loss. It is a shame people don't think more of them when they make such silly accusations."

"Is that Miss Fitzgerald's official line on the case?"

"There is no case," Annie snapped. "Miss Fitzgerald is recuperating with a broken foot at home."

"Then she has plenty of time to read the papers and see what all the town is talking about."

Annie shook her head.

"You are grasping at straws. Who started these rumours, anyway?"

"Ah, my sources must remain confidential," the reporter grinned. "Let it just be said that they were in a position to know the truth."

"I wish you would all let poor Mr Graves rest in peace," Annie sighed.

She was just walking away when the reporter called out to her.

"Ever wonder what happened to old Mr Graves? He died at his desk too, you know. Coincidence or the tell-tale mark of a murderer?"

Annie stopped in her tracks and found herself turning back to the reporter. The reporter tugged the brim of his hat as a mark of farewell and disappeared back among the bushes, clearly staking out the unfortunate Graves.

Annie hurried down the road feeling a little shaken. No one had mentioned the senior Mr Graves before. He had been dead over twenty years and probably most people had forgotten about him, but if he had died in the same way as his son, then the matter did require investigating. Was there more to this matter than met the eye? But, if this was the cause of Mr Erikson's suspicions, why had he not mentioned this before?

Annie was very glad she could hand over this confusing state of affairs to Clara as soon as she reached home. There were too many loose ends and, just perhaps, the Graves family was a little too light-hearted about the death of Isaac. She had not seen much sign of mourning, except from the distressed Julia. Was that a sign of guilt or simply stoicism? Annie found all this wondering was giving her a headache. She went to buy some apples and butter. Apple crumble did not cause this sort of confusion,

and right now Annie was longing to get back into the safe
orderliness of her kitchen.

Chapter Seven

Herbert Phinn sat at the Fitzgeralds' dining table and looked down at the last will and testament of Isaac Graves. Herbert was a chemist by training, a jolly good one too, but he had a passion for handwriting and had become quite the expert in fraudulent penmanship. It was a sideline, but one that had earned him more acclaim than his day job testing common household products for hazardous chemicals.

Herbert had known Tommy Fitzgerald since they were both at school. They were chalk and cheese, but in a way that worked to the benefit of both. They complemented each other. Clara liked Herbert for his frank, happy nature. He saw solutions rather than problems in any given situation. A man whose glass was always half full and with the promise of being refilled at any moment. Herbert usually couldn't resist a problematic will. Identifying fraud was one of his favourite aspects of these sorts of cases. It required a keen eye and an understanding of the victim. But, right at that moment, Herbert was struggling because he was being distracted.

"Can you hear that whining sound?" he asked the others. The noise had been bothering him since he had arrived. "I first heard it coming up your path. Could it be a baby left alone?"

Herbert was soft-hearted, and the thought of any living thing in distress troubled him. Clara cocked her head and listened. She had noticed the odd whining sound too, but had thought it was the wind in the chimney. Tommy merely shrugged.

"Sounds like a cat to me."

Herbert shook his head, looking upset and a touch cross.

"Have you not seen how women leave their children all alone? I see prams left outside shops, and infants left home on their own. Do you know how many cases there are every year of children under five swallowing dangerous household chemicals when left alone? It would make you shudder. I had a case only last week. A child had consumed a bottle of household cleaner and died. The manufacturers had scented it with roses to make it more appealing and the child thought it was something sweet to drink. I was called to discover how much of the stuff would be fatal and whether the manufacturers were at fault for not putting a warning label on the bottle," Herbert grimaced. "Perhaps the manufacturer could have been more cautious, but the mother had left the child home on its own while she went shopping. She returned two hours later to find the infant in a terrible condition. Surely she bears some responsibility for the accident?"

"I dare say," Clara said gently, trying to appease the clearly distraught Herbert. "But mothers will claim they must go out and sometimes they cannot take a child on errands."

"It is unforgiveable," Herbert insisted. "It has played on my mind ever since."

He turned his attention back to the whining noise outside.

"One of your neighbours has left a child unattended," he declared.

"I doubt that, most of them are too old to have young

children," but Clara was also now wondering what that odd noise was.

"I must investigate. Excuse me," Herbert rose from the table and left the two siblings who were unable to follow.

Clara glanced at her brother.

"Herbert gets very upset about these things," Tommy said.

"I don't blame him. Too many children die in accidents because of a lack of supervision."

"But it really must be a cat?" Tommy was distracted by the sound of Herbert forcing himself into the large bush outside the dining room window. "What is he doing now?"

Herbert emerged from the bush looking like a wildman, with twigs tangled in his hair and his glasses askew. One of Clara's passing neighbours gave him an odd look. Then Herbert vanished again and they heard the front door open and close.

Herbert appeared at the door of the dining room with a bundle under his arm. For one awful moment, with the bundle almost hidden by Herbert's jacket, Clara thought a baby had been abandoned on her doorstep. Such things did happen, though never to her before. But when Herbert pulled the bundle out from under his jacket it was not a human infant. It was a small black dog with extremely curly hair.

"It was whimpering in the bushes. It's all skin and bones," Herbert placed the dog on the seat of the chair he had just vacated and they all looked at the scruffy thing.

It didn't look very appealing with its tatty overgrown coat, mud caked on its paws and no sign of eyes among the fur of its face.

"I think it is a poodle," Herbert said. "Can't tell until you clip the hair."

Clara sighed. Yet another of life's waifs and strays had been deposited at her door. She stared at the shivering black thing, trying to make out which bit was dog and which was hair.

"Get it a plate of bread and milk from the pantry, Herbert," Tommy instructed. "Then we can get back to the matter at hand. We can ring the dog warden later."

Herbert went to his task. The dog sat on the chair where it had been placed looking utterly dejected. Clara knew how it felt. She had been that way since her foot was run over. She wondered where it had come from. It was clearly the sort of small dog posh ladies liked to carry around with them. It probably dined on caviar and venison most days when at home. How it had ended up here and in such a state was a mystery. Perhaps it had been stolen and then escaped its kidnappers?

Herbert returned with a dish and placed it under the poor creature's nose. The small dog sniffed uncertainly for a moment, then consumed the entire plateful with relish. Milk dripped off its curly mouth hair as it licked the plate clean. Its meal completed, it hopped off the chair and went to a chaise longue it had spotted in the far corner of the room. It jumped onto the chaise and settled down in a curled ball to sleep.

"Make yourself at home, won't you?" Tommy laughed.

The little dog was already snoring.

Herbert reacquired his seat and pulled Isaac Graves' will towards him.

"At last I can concentrate," he said with a sigh. He pulled a magnifying glass from his pocket and started to examine the writing.

It had not been difficult to find genuine samples of Mr Graves' handwriting. Mr Erikson had been most helpful in sorting out old letters and documents that Isaac had definitely written himself. They also held his signature, the key factor for deciding if the will was a fake or not.

Clara felt uncomfortable watching Herbert work. She felt as if her gaze was rushing him, suggesting she was impatient. She was, but she didn't want to show it. She would have talked to Tommy but that would be distracting. Instead she ran through the descriptions Annie had given her of the Graves family in her mind, and thought of Mr Graves' wife who she had met personally. None of them struck her as killers, but there was definitely some sort of disharmony in the family. Genuine or fake, Isaac's will demonstrated that discord. And who had let slip the rumours of Graves being possibly murdered? She hoped it was not Mr Erikson. Such indiscretion would be troubling in a solicitor.

She was mulling on this when the doorbell rang. With no Annie at home to answer it, Clara rose using the stick she had been loaned by the doctor and went to answer it herself. On her doorstep was a rather troubled looking undertaker.

"Mr Clark," Clara greeted him warmly enough. She did not blame him for the accident.

Mr Clark removed his hat and clutched it before him in both hands.

"Might I come in, Miss Fitzgerald?"

Clara suggested they head for the parlour and Mr Clark was good enough to shut the door for her as he came in. They settled in two armchairs before the fire, Mr Clark still looking frightened to death. Clara waited patiently for him to speak.

"How is your foot, Miss Fitzgerald?"

"Sore, but it will heal. I do not blame you for the accident, Mr Clark. Horses have their own minds, after all."

"First time old Bill has shown himself up like that," Mr Clark shook his head sadly. "He has pulled hearses for me these last ten years. A fine horse. Normally as calm as anything. That was why I was so perplexed. I thought perhaps he was ill. But I found the cause, all right, when I got him home."

"Was he ill?"

"Not as such. Some fool had placed a thumb tack under his harness. When he moved in a certain way it would prick into his skin and spook him," Mr Clark wrung his hat through his hands. "I don't have polite words for any person who could treat a horse so badly. Not to mention it put me in an awkward position."

"Do you think someone wished to hurt your business?" Clara asked, her curiosity piqued. Someone had deliberately arranged for old Bill to become uncontrollable, but why?

"I couldn't say for certain. I am on pretty good terms with the other funeral directors in the town. We don't tend to clash. It also means that someone must have snuck into my stable yard after Bill was harnessed up. I tend not to leave him too long in harness, as he gets restless. It is one of the last jobs my boys do, getting old Bill ready."

"You surely don't think one of your employees was responsible?"

"No. They have all been with me for years," Mr Clark sighed forlornly. "You should have seen poor Bill's back where the tack had cut into him. He is jumpy about having any harness put on him now."

"I don't blame him. What a shame horses can't talk, then he could tell us who was behind this cruel trick."

"I can't be dealing with people who would hurt a dumb animal in such a way," Mr Clark concluded. "I really have taken up too much of your time. I just wanted to apologise and explain what had happened."

"No need, Mr Clark. I truly understand it was an accident."

"You are too good, Miss Fitzgerald. I would also like to offer you a discount on any future funeral you care to arrange with us. We will do it for three quarters of the usual price."

Clara found the offer rather disturbing.

"Let us hope I don't have the opportunity to take you up on that offer for a long time," Clara told him with a smile as she ushered him out of the house.

By the time she returned to the dining room Herbert had finished his perusal of the will and was chatting with Tommy.

"Well?" Clara asked, looking from one man to the

other.

"It is one of those situations where I can't be perfectly certain," Herbert said, tapping the will with one thoughtful finger. "But, I would say this is an extremely good fake."

Clara sat down heavily in a chair.

"But you can't be certain?"

"Whoever created this will was very familiar with the way Mr Graves wrote, specifically the way he used language and how he structured his sentences. Wills are rather formulaic at the best of times, but you can see patterns emerge. For instance, Mr Graves was very fond of using dashes rather than commas to break up long sentences. I can see this in all his documents and in the wording of the will."

"But then, surely that makes the will genuine?"

"Ah!" Herbert held up a finger. "You would think so. But Mr Graves had a very useful habit which our forger overlooked faking. I believe Mr Graves was a 'nib-licker'."

Tommy raised an eyebrow at the phrase.

"It is a habit people develop when they use pencils a lot. Certain papers do not take pencil marks so well as others and licking a pencil tip can help to make a more distinctive mark. Pencil lickers tend to transfer the habit unconsciously when they write with a pen."

"How does this help?" Clara asked, trying to remember if she had ever licked a pencil tip.

"When you lick the nib of a pen you leave behind saliva that dilutes the ink for a few strokes. It also has the potential to make the ink go further, because it revives dry material. Mr Graves tended to lick his pen nib when the ink was running low. A habit he was familiar with from using a pencil that refused to lay a decent mark. I can see where he licked his pen nib when I use the magnifying glass. I can see where the ink has becoming diluted on the start of words. Equally, I can see patches of text where he was running out of ink, licked the nib by habit to gain a few more letters, then refilled the pen.

Refilling the reservoir of a fountain pen is such a nuisance when you are in the middle of something. If you can eke out a few more words before the pen gives up, you usually try."

"But the faker did not?"

"I can see the marks I have described in several places on the documents you say are genuine. But not on the will. The writer of the will was not a nib-licker."

"It is a minor thing, though," Clara said. "Perhaps, because it was an important will, Mr Graves made the effort to keep his pen full?"

"Perhaps," Herbert admitted. "I found something in the signature too. It was quite curious. The sort of thing that raises alarm bells."

Herbert moved the will towards Clara and offered her the magnifying glass.

"Look how perfect the signature is, how smoothly written."

Clara looked.

"Yes?"

"No one writes their signature that nicely. We sign things quickly and automatically. This signature was carefully drawn. See how dense the ink is? It is because the pen was held in position for so long and the signature written slowly. It is one of the warning signs that a signature has been forged."

Clara studied the paper again. She thought she saw what Herbert meant, but it was all very unclear.

"So, just possibly, we have a forged will?" she clarified.

"Indeed. Though, you would need more than those two observations to prove anything. It is a very good copy."

Clara looked at the will again. Was this the first clue to something suspicious occurring in Mr Graves' life? But if that was the case, how had the forger gained access to a safe supposedly only two men knew the combination to? And where was the real will? Had it been destroyed or merely hidden? Clara studied the paper a bit longer and

felt suddenly more hopeful. Perhaps there was more to
Mr Erikson's suspicions than mere rumour? It was time
to take this case very seriously.

Chapter Eight

Annie gave a shriek and almost dropped the apple crumble she had slaved over all afternoon. Fortunately, she was pragmatic by nature and, despite her surprise, the pan remained firmly clasped in her hands as she hurried to the dining room. Clara had just risen awkwardly from her chair and was attempting to discover what was the matter, when Annie appeared in the doorway.

"Are you all right?"

"There is a great big black rat in my kitchen!" Annie declared, looking more furious at the intrusion by vermin into her orderly domain than scared.

She was just putting the crumble on the table when she gave another cry.

"There it is, running past the table leg! It's jumped on the chaise!"

"Oh, that's just Bramble," Tommy stated, waving a hand in the general direction of the dog.

"Bramble? It has a name now?" Clara asked.

"Well, it was found in a bush tangled in brambles, hence..."

"There are no brambles in my garden," Clara said robustly.

Tommy gave her a look that suggested she was

hopelessly misguided on that front.

"In any case, I named the dog."

"That's a dog!" Annie stared at the mass of muddy fur that was the aforementioned Bramble.

"We think it is a poodle," Clara added. "Herbert found it in the front garden."

"And is it staying?" Annie asked in a sharp tone. Visions of muddy paws on her clean sheets and mysteriously stolen lamb chops had sprung to mind.

"We thought we would try to trace Bramble's owner," Tommy answered, trying to avoid Annie's glare. "The Home for Lost Dogs is such a cold, lonely place. To ship Bramble there seemed rather… unkind."

"Once you named it there was no going back," Clara sighed at her brother. "You always did love dogs."

"And if you can't trace the owner?" Annie knew the answer to that one already.

Tommy just looked sheepish.

"As I thought," Annie glowered at Bramble. The small dog wagged its matted tail at her and gave a friendly yap. "Well, at least you could give it a trim and find out if it is a boy or a girl. A bath would probably be a good idea too."

"At once. Straight after dinner," Clara promised, glad to see Annie's temper assuaged.

They settled down to apple crumble, Bramble watching them with a keen eye from the chaise longue.

"Annie, I think it is time we talked with Mr Erikson again," Clara got back to business. "He needs to know Herbert's findings on the will and we also need to try and pin down a timeline of events. Mrs Hatton states she left around quarter to eleven, that leaves an hour and a quarter before the discovery of poor Mr Graves' body. Who had access to his office during that time?"

"I think I can handle that," Annie said stoutly. She was beginning to get quite good at this detective lark. "I shall pop in to see him when I go to buy the fish for Friday."

"I think I shall ask the widow, Grace Graves, to pay

another call and gently air out my suspicions. She may be able to offer an insight into the Graves' family affairs. Also, we now know that Mr Graves' will was made in favour of his sister Julia."

"She was the only one who looked truly upset by his death," Annie added.

"Which is somewhat curious if she was behind the forged will and, subsequently, his death. Unless there is something more complicated about this drama than we have yet to discover."

"Then there is the matter of the sabotage of Mr Clark's horse," Tommy said, helping himself to seconds from the crumble dish. "Unless we consider that a completely coincidental occurrence."

"That bothers me too," Clara admitted. "But, if it was deliberate, I simply can't see the purpose."

"Unless someone was trying to draw attention to the matter of Mr Graves' death," Annie suggested.

Clara and Tommy looked at her to expand on that statement.

"Well, say you had suspicions about Mr Graves' sad demise, but had no proof. Causing a little chaos at the funeral would draw attention and perhaps offer a means of attracting the press. After all, such a strange incident would have the reporters hovering around the Graves family like flies. It is not as though we have a lot of news in Brighton."

"And once you had the attention of the press, you might slip in a word or two of your suspicions?" Tommy elaborated.

"Yes. But no one need know it was you who had made the suggestion, because you had a perfectly legitimate reason of speaking with a reporter. It would avoid bringing suspicion down on yourself."

"And, if you thought the killer was one of your family, it would not be such a bad idea to keep your fears as secret as possible," Clara added.

"Precisely," Annie looked deeply satisfied with herself.

"You know, Annie, you are becoming quite the detective," Clara grinned at her. "I think it's about time we learned a little more about Mr Graves. Did he have enemies outside his family, for instance? He was involved in a lot of societies and charities. I can make enquiries with the Pavilion Committee. The rest I will have to leave up to you."

Annie gave a little sigh.

"I wanted to wash all the table linen tomorrow," she said, a tad grumpily.

"I'm sure we can manage that between us, old girl," Tommy volunteered himself and Clara.

Annie gave them a look which suggested she had severe doubts about their domestic abilities, but there was nothing else to be done. There was a crime that needed investigating and she was the only one able to do it. Even if it did interrupt her cleaning routine.

~~~*~~~

Mr Erikson sat at his desk staring at his rapidly cooling cup of tea. Mr Erikson felt old today, though many would argue he was still in the prime of life. He was fit and healthy, with no real aches and pains to complain of. He had many years ahead of him as yet. But that could not stop him from feeling old, from feeling that a great deal of time had passed without him even noticing it going by. Where had that young man full of ideas and ambitions gone to? He had expected so much from life, and he had achieved a great deal of those expectations, but now he wondered what was left? What did he have to look forward to or aim towards? In truth, Mr Erikson missed his business partner immensely.

He had rather taken Isaac's presence for granted. He had been such a feature of everyday life for the last thirty or so years, that Mr Erikson had hardly given it a thought. They said 'good morning' to each other at eight o'clock precisely, then retreated to their respective offices with any messages their secretary had collected for them. At midday, Mr Erikson roused his partner for a drink and a sandwich. It was the part of the day Erikson really enjoyed. They would discuss work, ironing out tricky problems between themselves and relaxing. Then it was back to the office for the afternoon. Sometime around five Erikson would call it a day and head for home. He would say his farewells to his colleague who, invariably, would still be working. With any luck Isaac would just make it home in time for dinner. Then he would be off to one of his many committee meetings. Erikson would spend the evening relaxing at home with a glass of brandy, occasionally thinking of his tireless colleague and finding the thought of being able to rest of an evening all the more enjoyable because he knew Isaac would be many hours before returning to his bed.

Erikson felt guilty about that thought now. How he had chuckled at his friend's ceaseless endeavours. Tutted quietly to himself and mumbled how Isaac would run himself into an early grave, though not really taking the thought seriously. And now Isaac was dead, perhaps in part because of his inability to rest, and Erikson felt as if he should have done more to save him.

Erikson, in the last few days, had begun to doubt his original suspicions. Voicing them aloud to Miss Fitzgerald's agent had made them sound rather ludicrous. Perhaps, after all, it had been a natural death? Perhaps Erikson had wished it otherwise to try and assuage his own guilt at not being firmer with Isaac? If only he had insisted on him leaving the office at the same time as he did. Or, maybe, he had been a little too keen to deposit any will related work on his partner? Had he contributed to Isaac's unfortunate death?

Annie found Mr Erikson immersed in these guilt-riddled thoughts. The legal documents he was supposed to be perusing for a client remained untouched on his desk, and a whole hour had ticked by without him doing anything but fret about the past. Annie felt sorry for him, recognising a man who had suddenly been struck by the full force of his grief.

"Miss Green, I am pleased to see you again," Mr Erikson roused himself and offered Annie a chair.

"I brought back the will and the documents you loaned me," Annie said, producing a cardboard filing folder from her large shopping basket.

"What did your handwriting expert make of them?" Mr Erikson said, with little hope in his tone.

"He thinks the will is a forgery."

Mr Erikson was so thrown by this news that he actually gaped at Annie. Then he recovered himself.

"He said that?"

"Yes. But it is a very good forgery, nonetheless. He wrote out a brief report for you, outlining his conclusions," Annie produced three sheets of paper containing Herbert's slightly scrawled handwriting. He had written his report before leaving the Fitzgerald house the day before.

Erikson took the papers with trembling fingers. Could it be he was not as foolish as he first imagined?

"Of course, we still have the problem of how someone could gain access to the safe where the will was kept," Annie interrupted his thoughts, trying to let him down gently.

"The safe is kept across the hall in our reference room. Here, let me show you," Erikson rose and escorted Annie across the hall.

The reference room contained a full library of legal texts and a series of filing cabinets in the one space. The safe, a compact green affair with the brand name of Small and Co. embossed on it, sat in one corner, slightly hidden by a bookcase.

"I suppose anyone could access it once they were past our secretary downstairs," Mr Erikson mused.

Annie bent down and examined the safe. It looked pretty solid to her, but appearances could be deceptive. After all, it only took the knowledge of a series of numbers to render this safe completely useless for hiding valuables in.

"Who knows the combination?" she asked.

"Myself and Isaac. I have never given it to anyone else."

"But Mr Graves might have?"

Erikson shook his head. His earlier excitement was dissolving once more into uncertainty.

"Isaac would not give the combination out freely."

"Was it perhaps written down somewhere, that a person might find it that way?"

"No. We had memorised it. We had used it for so many years that the odds of forgetting it were extremely slim."

Annie imagined what Clara would say about having the same safe combination for years and years. Yes, the possibility of someone learning that combination was becoming more and more feasible.

"Did any of Mr Graves' family visit the office?"

"From time to time," Mr Erikson nodded. "Though not Mrs Graves, the widow."

"No?"

"In all my time here, I think she has visited the office once, perhaps twice. She resented Isaac's work and refused to endorse it by calling here."

"So there is the possibility of someone coming into this room and opening the safe without anyone knowing? Possibly after an appointment with Mr Graves?"

Erikson mulled on this a while before answering;

"Yes."

"Now, the morning Mr Graves passed, Mrs Hatton states she left around ten forty-five."

"I confirmed that with our secretary downstairs. Everyone has to go past her to leave the building," Erikson said.

"Around what time did you hear a door opening and closing?"

Erikson paused. He was not sure, if he was honest. It

had been such a casual noise, one which, at the time, he had only half heard.

"It was at least a half hour before I went to call on Isaac."

"Around eleven thirty?"

"Yes, something like that."

"Did your secretary see anyone else enter the building between Mrs Hatton leaving and midday?"

"No."

"Then, how could someone else get in undetected?"

Mr Erikson was silent again for some time. His suspicions of murder rapidly came undone when the logistics were considered. The will might have been forged, there seemed evidence for it, but that did not mean Isaac's death was unnatural.

"The only other entrance to the building is via our backyard," he said after a long time spent thinking. "It has no access to the road and is completely enclosed. In fact, it has long been a bone of contention, as it means having to carry our dust bins through the property when they need to be emptied."

"Determined intruders don't need doors to enter a building," Annie pointed out. "When I lived at home, our neighbours' farm was once burgled. The culprits climbed in through a skylight. No one had imagined that was even possible."

"I see your point. A person could scale the wall and then enter by the back door. It is not kept locked during the day. Once inside they could climb the stairs without being noticed," Mr Erikson brightened. "But at least it could not be a woman. A woman could not climb that wall in her skirts."

"Don't be so certain," Annie replied, thinking of some of the escapades Clara had gotten herself into.

"This is all very disturbing," Mr Erikson looked worried again.

"Have you found the missing documents Mrs Hatton mentioned?"

"No. That is deeply troubling. I can only assume the person who I heard entering the building stole them. Do you suppose they killed Isaac too?"

"Hard to tell," Annie admitted.

"It is odd, but when I first had my suspicions all I wanted was for someone to believe me and prove me right. Now I keep wishing I was wrong," Mr Erikson grew deeply sad. "I want justice for Isaac, but at what price Miss Green? What have I stumbled upon?"

"The truth," Annie said gently. "And that is what it is. Don't mean its pleasant, but we wouldn't be anywhere if we ignored it."

"I hope you are right," Mr Erikson sighed forlornly. "I do so hope you are right."

Chapter Nine

Mrs Graves looked worried when she called to see Clara again.

"Is there something wrong with the papers I signed?" she asked anxiously.

"No, nothing like that. I had another matter I wished to discuss with you," Clara explained, showing her guest into the parlour. She offered her freshly toasted crumpets, but Mrs Graves declined. She looked extremely pale and her appearance had an air of neglect about it. She seemed to be suffering greatly over the death of her husband.

"I'm sorry to trouble you again," Clara said, feeling bad that she had summoned the woman once more, only so she might impart more bad news. "I wouldn't have done so had it not been quite urgent."

Mrs Graves nodded her head.

"I was sorting out his wardrobe. I thought he would like it if some of his clothes went to a good cause. There are charities always asking for old clothes."

"There are indeed," Clara sympathised. "He was a good man, your husband."

"Yes. But very busy. It can be hard being married to a good man, Miss Fitzgerald. He always had time for the poor and the unfortunate, but very little for me," Mrs

Graves smiled forlornly. "My mother said I was a fool for marrying him, I suppose she was right."

"She didn't approve of Mr Graves?"

"Not precisely. She could see he would look after me and he had no real vices. But he was a man who lived for his work, even when I first knew him it was always that way. She said I would be a lonely woman if I married him."

"I'm sorry to hear that."

"I made my choice," Mrs Graves shrugged, as if that was the end of the matter. "What did you wish to see me about?"

"It is a rather delicate matter," Clara admitted, feeling she was walking on eggshells. "There has been some concern over your husband's will."

"What sort of concern?" Mrs Graves suddenly perked up.

"There is a possibility that the will may have been forged."

Mrs Graves suddenly sat very upright. She looked surprised, but also pleased.

"Forged? I was always confused at the nature of his will. Leaving everything to Julia Graves seemed decidedly odd."

"Was he very close to Julia?"

"I suppose you could say that," Mrs Graves mused. "They were on some of the same committees. They shared philanthropic ideals. Even so, we were all startled by the contents of his will. But now you say it may have been forged?"

"There are indications of that, yes," Clara said. "But we will need to look into the matter further before being certain."

"Could Julia have done this?"

"We cannot draw any conclusions just yet."

"I can't deny it would be to my advantage if the will was a fake," Mrs Graves had brightened considerably. "Isaac's death has left me in quite a bind. The will was a shock and left matters even worse."

"Had you doubts about the will already?"

"It had troubled me, but I can't say I had doubts. Isaac could have his odd whims, though to virtually cut out everyone but Julia seemed drastic. I found myself wondering what I had done to deserve such treatment. I know his mother was deeply distressed."

"Can you tell me a little more about the relationship between Mr Graves and his family?"

"In what sense?"

"Did they all get along? Were there ever disagreements?"

Mrs Graves looked away into the fireplace, thinking back to the past.

"In recent years I have kept my distance from the Graves family. They can be… possessive. They saw Isaac as belonging to them and my claims upon him were very much second rate. We did the usual thing of seeing each other at Christmas, but otherwise I involved myself as little as possible with the family," Mrs Graves paused. "Isaac did not talk much about them, either. But then, we often only saw each other at dinner and it was usually a rushed affair. I do recall him getting hot under the collar over his mother. She had placed pressure on him over some family matter. He didn't elaborate on the subject, but he felt a tad used and rather under-appreciated. That was some months back."

"Do the Graves women have any financial provisions aside from what your husband gave them?"

"A few odd investments, but nothing that could keep them in the style they are accustomed to. Really, Isaac was of no good to them dead, well, at least not now with the new will…"

Mrs Graves trailed off and the unspoken thought hung in the air.

"But the old will would have provided for them?"

"I believe so. Isaac did like to talk about wills, they were his specialty. And I recall he had made one that would see his mother and sisters amply provided for, for the rest of their days. He had made some substantial investments on their behalf. I too was well provided for. That was why the new will was such a shock. All those investments and bonds going to one sister alone? It seemed very peculiar."

"And very unlike Mr Graves?"

"Well… Now you mention it, it was not the way Isaac behaved. He took his responsibilities very seriously."

"That is what I thought. Tell me, did you notice how Julia took the news of the will?"

"She was not at the reading. She had gone to bed with a headache," Mrs Graves gave a smile. "That does seem rather odd under the circumstances, doesn't it?"

It did. But it was hardly conclusive.

So far Clara had avoided suggesting that Mr Graves had been murdered, she hoped to keep that idea firmly out of Mrs Graves' head. But Mrs Graves was not a stupid woman and she had lived with a specialist in wills long enough to know that forgery often went hand-in-hand with murder. She gave Clara an assessing look.

"You think someone killed my husband?" she said.

"I have not made up my mind on the subject," Clara hedged her bets.

"It is a curious idea. The coroner found nothing to suggest it. No poisons, or such, though I suppose he was not particularly looking for them. There was nothing that might suggest the cause of death, which did seem a rather peculiar coincidence," Mrs Graves raised her eyebrows in a telling look. She was waiting for Clara to ask, and she obliged.

"What coincidence?"

"Mr Graves' father died in nearly the exact same circumstances. They found him slumped at his desk. The coroner could find no cause for that, either."

Clara's ears pricked up. Annie had mentioned something about a strange coincidence right before rushing off to make apple crumble. She had not elaborated on the matter and Clara had forgotten, which was a shame, as a father and son dying in the exact same way many years apart did tend to make a detective's instincts tingle.

"How long ago was this?"

"Let me see. Isaac was in his late twenties, so it must have been the 1890s. I can't remember the precise date, but I imagine I could find out."

"Please do," Clara pressed. "I would like to compare the two cases."

Mrs Graves was looking extremely pleased with herself as she left the appointment. Whether this was because she was finally on the path to finding justice for her husband, or because his last will might prove fraudulent, Clara could not say.

Clara eased herself back into her favourite armchair. Her foot was very sore and she pulled off the house slippers she had worn during her chat with Mrs Graves. It had seemed rather oafish to sit around with just stockinged feet during a formal interview.

There was a scampering noise and the small black dog, now named Bramble, sprang onto her lap. Clara gave an exasperated sigh; the dog really had no manners. Bramble shoved his little face into hers (she had learned he was a 'he' while bathing and clipping him) and licked her vigorously. She pushed him away, though he gave her an offended look. Bramble leapt to the floor and tore off with one of the discarded slippers. Clara started to call after him, but it was no use. He was too fast and far too mischievous to listen to her, though, she had to admit, he did have a certain charm after his inexpert clip. Tommy was drafting a notice for the local paper to see if someone was missing the little blighter.

Clara's foot was just starting to ease when the doorbell rang again, this time rather frantically. Or so it seemed, for doorbells are rather bland as noises go. But Clara received the impression that someone wanted her rather urgently. She hobbled to the door and found a distressed

Mrs Hatton just outside.

"Miss Fitzgerald?"

"Yes?"

"I spoke with your agent just the other day. Did she tell you about my troubles?"

"Annie tells me everything," Clara assured her, even if that was not quite accurate when Annie's mind turned to cooking. "Would you like to come in?"

The flustered woman did just that. Clara would have liked to have offered her a cup of tea, to try and calm her clearly jangled nerves, but she was in too much pain to stumble to the kitchen to make it. The best she could do was offer Mrs Hatton some shortbread biscuits that had been left on the table after Mrs Graves' visit.

"It is just terrible, terrible!" Mrs Hatton accepted a biscuit absentmindedly. "Your agent told you about my dealings with Mr Graves?"

"She explained he was drawing up divorce papers for you."

"Yes, that is it precisely. And did she explain they had gone missing?"

"Yes, and she also went to Mr Erikson and informed him that certain important papers appeared to have vanished. He is endeavouring to find them."

"Well you can tell him to stop bothering," Mrs Hatton said miserably. "I know where they are. In my husband's possession to be exact."

Clara was stunned.

"Mr Hatton stole the papers?"

"It would seem so. Do you realise what this means?"

Clara did. Had Mr Hatton stumbled on the papers by chance in the dead man's office after sneaking in through the back door of Erikson and Graves' building, or was he a murderer? In either case, it was entirely probable he was the mysterious door opener and had also encountered a dead body, and then failed to report it.

"I was not aware your husband knew about the divorce yet?"

"Nor was I. I was keeping silent until the papers were drawn up. Then I was going to hand them to him and demand he set me free. Oh, Miss Fitzgerald! The argument we had was just so horrid. We both said things... He was so hurt. I had not expected that."

Clara wondered how the woman could have failed to expect that, considering she had been secretly arranging for a divorce behind her husband's back.

"Has Mr Hatton said what he wishes to do concerning the divorce papers?" she asked instead.

"He wants to forget them. Pretend it never happened. He has made it pretty plain he will not even countenance a divorce. It is all so awful. I felt like I would die as he shouted at me."

Clara offered the woman another biscuit, perceiving her as one of the world's great dramatists. The sort who finds mountains in molehills. No doubt it had been an awful morning, but had the woman not been so cloak and dagger with the matter none of this would have happened. At some point she would have given Mr Hatton the papers and he would have reacted in exactly the way she described, probably mainly out of shock and affront.

"When matters calm down, perhaps Mr Hatton will be prepared to discuss a divorce," she suggested.

"He will never hear of it! He said as much," Mrs Hatton flapped her hands and biscuit crumbs went everywhere. "I blame Mr Graves, you understand. Had he put those papers in a safe place before dying none of this would have happened."

Clara felt that was rather unfair. She doubted the man had intended to die so inconveniently.

"I will need to speak with Mr Hatton."

"Surely not!" Mrs Hatton flapped faster. "If he was to learn I had spoken with a private detective he would be infuriated!"

"But you did not hire me. I spoke with you on behalf of a completely independent client, and it was not concerning your divorce either. However, legal documents were stolen from Mr Graves' office, that is a very serious crime. And, as I cannot imagine Mr Graves allowing such a thing were he to be aware of the matter, I have to conclude that your husband entered the office after Mr Graves was deceased."

Or had made him deceased, Clara added to herself, though the exact motive was vague. Deflected fury at the man helping his wife, perhaps? Even if the man was merely doing his professional duty.

"Will my husband be in trouble?" Mrs Hatton clutched a fist to her mouth in horror at the idea.

"There is that possibility. He has committed a crime, after all. But Mr Erikson will have to decide whether to press charges. Now, are you fit to go home and inform Mr Hatton he must see me at once?"

Mrs Hatton wasn't certain she was fit. She had had a trying morning. All her future plans had crumbled around her and she now felt deeply uneasy about speaking with her husband.

"No. I couldn't."

"Is he at work today?"

"Yes. He is the owner of the Great Britain Charabanc Company. He has lots to deal with and will be in his office."

"Then I shall ring his office, I presume it is on the 'phone?"

Mrs Hatton nodded that it was.

"This is just so dreadful," she shook her head. "He will know I came to you."

There was no way of getting around that fact, but Clara had to speak with Mr Hatton. At the very least he might be an extremely important witness.

"I shall be discreet," it was the best she could promise.

Mrs Hatton dithered for a few more moments, then conceded that there was nothing else to be done. Her secret had been discovered.

"I suppose Mr Hatton somehow learned of your plans?

Else how would he have known to go to Mr Graves' office?" Clara speculated as Mrs Hatton made to leave.

"Do you think he was following me?" Mrs Hatton asked aghast, as if it was the most appalling idea she had ever heard.

"It is difficult to imagine otherwise," Clara admitted.

Mrs Hatton left looking as though her whole world had crumbled down around her. Clara felt sorry for her, after all. But she felt even more sorry for Mr Graves, who, it was beginning to seem, might have been an innocent victim caught in the middle of a domestic feud. Was Mr Hatton a murderer? Or simply extremely lucky to have stumbled into Mr Graves' office when the gentleman was already dead? And what of Mrs Graves' revelation that her husband's father had died in the exact same manner? What a tangled web people weaved!

Chapter Ten

Annie read the address on the slip of paper Clara had given her and gave a slight shudder. The Ladies' House of Reform was not a place she had ever anticipated entering. Brighton had shot to fame in the Georgian period when a certain prince decided that it was an ideal place to build a summer house and to spend his holidays. The summer house proved to be a gargantuan pavilion, decorated in a style some considered akin to the great Indian palaces, and others equated to a madman's fantasy. Love it or hate it, the Pavilion was a symbol of the rise of Brighton. With the endorsement of a prince, Brighton became a hotspot for every lord and lady, court follower, or those hopeful to infiltrate themselves into the royal circle. Brighton expanded to accommodate them all. Quite frankly, the passion that Prince George IV showed for the town had turned it from a sleepy fishing village into the holiday resort it was today. Helped, of course, by the news that Brighton's waters contained beneficial properties and could cure almost anything – at least according to the eighteenth century doctors who prescribed it.

However, it was not just the rich and the nobility who descended to Brighton in the season; in their wake came those hoping to make money from the wealthy and gullible. Some of these hangers-on provided legitimate enough business to their well-to-do clients, others, however, dallied in the illegal. Gambling, drugs and, of course, prostitution.

Like any town, Brighton had its resident brigade of red ladies, but the 'season' swelled their numbers out of all proportion. At the height of Brighton's fame, it could be challenging to find a respectable lady on the streets at all. Matters were only made worse by the creation of a military camp just outside the town. Men in uniform, shortly due to sail off and fight Napoleon, were all too tempting game. The professional women were bad enough, but, like all military camps, the one outside Brighton attracted naive young girls overawed by a handsome uniform. They came with romantic ideas that were soon dashed if they were foolish enough to allow themselves to be sweet-talked into abandoning their virtue. Once fallen they joined the ranks of the many other women of the night haunting the streets.

As a girl, Annie had read Pride and Prejudice by Jane Austen. In the novel, the silly-brained Lydia Bennet runs off with a soldier and comes close to joining the ranks of fallen women. Austen's description of the feather-brained camp followers, naive girls who loved uniforms and lived for dancing, was probably not so far from the truth. Lydia Bennet was lucky enough to have her family save her, many girls were not.

All this had added up to one thing by the Victorian period; Brighton had become notorious for prostitution. Perhaps not such a problem with the debauched Georges on the throne, but when Victoria took over, she took one look at the Pavilion and the town surrounding it and refused to have anything to do with it. Brighton lost its royal patronage and slipped into somewhat of a decline. But the women remained; starving on street corners, scaring innocent passers-by, giving the town a seedy atmosphere. The civic fathers toyed with the idea of simply expelling them all. The more charitable among them felt that many of the women were victims of circumstance and should be offered a second chance. Thus the Ladies' House of Reform was founded, to take in street women and help them to return to normal life. In its near 100 years of operation it had succumbed to the odd scandal, (one vicar had been a little too keen in his patronage) but, by and large, it had served a valuable purpose. And, although Brighton was now rather less inundated by ladies of the night, it still opened its doors to those wishing to change their fates and provided a safe haven for those 'Lydias' of the world.

Annie, however, felt deeply uncomfortable going near it. Despite its many noble and respectable benefactors, it was not a place where any self-respecting single woman wanted to be seen, less it be imagined she was seeking help within. Clara would no doubt have barely given it a thought, but Clara belonged to a bracket of society that few could really imagine dabbling in street prostitution. Annie, on the other hand, was a servant from a working class family. Just the sort of girl who could easily slip into night-work to make a little pocket money.

Annie was petrified that one of her friends, or just someone who knew her name, might see her going inside. She was so nervous that she loitered for half-an-hour at the greengrocer's shop opposite, trying to pluck up the courage to make her entrance. She ended up buying apples and onions and some extremely early rhubarb that had the look about it of something rather artificial. Finally cowed by her pointless purchases, she made up her mind, and tried to look completely innocent as she wandered across the road and knocked on the front door of the House. If anyone asked she would say she was delivering pamphlets for the local Church. That was a righteous enough reason to be going to a reform house, wasn't it?

The door was opened by a woman in a plain skirt and blouse, a tad out-of-date in style, but distinctly respectable. Annie gave a start as she realised she recognised the woman before her.

"Maud Binkley?"

"Annie Green! Why, I have not seen you since we did that stint together in the munitions factory," Maud Binkley smiled. She was a healthy looking young woman, the sort who might be found on a farm robustly milking cows. She had an open and friendly face that tended towards a ruddy complexion, much to the girl's embarrassment.

"What are you doing here?" Annie asked, still astonished to see someone she knew on the threshold of the Reform House.

"I work here," Maud chuckled. "Don't look so shocked! I haven't been playing on the streets personally."

Annie realised she must be looking aghast at Maud and pulled herself together.

"Can I come in? I am here on an errand."

"I didn't think you were after help," Maud winked rather mischievously.

Annie went pale, but followed the woman inside without another word. Maud led her into a small parlour that served as an office. There was a fire burning low in the grate and the room smelt of oil paint and floor polish. Maud offered her a chair.

"I look after the place Monday to Thursday," Maud explained. "Mainly just answering the door and watching over the girls. Oh, and all the paperwork," Maud waved a hand at a desk covered with papers. "Mrs Dobbs covers Fridays to Sundays. She doesn't believe in God, you see, so doesn't go to church on Sundays. It is the ideal arrangement."

"How did you end up here?" Annie asked, still feeling confused.

"I needed work after the war," Maud shrugged. "Mrs Dobbs knew my mother, she said a respectable and sensible girl was needed to oversee the place during the week. I have to be a bastion of propriety, you know. Not a hint of misbehaviour must ever surround me. I teach at the Sunday School, and the vicar thought I would be ideal for providing a sound and proper influence to these girls."

"Are you here alone?"

"Heavens, no! I mean, there are two teachers who come in to help educate the girls daily. Many can't read or write, and they often have no household skills. We aim to readjust the girls to normal life and find them legitimate work, often as servants. Knowing how to darn a sock and the best way to polish silver is just the start. We teach them to cook and clean, and naturally there is religious education. Though Mrs Dobbs does tend to wrinkle her nose when the subject is mentioned.

"Then there is the caretaker. I think he must be nearly eighty," Maud giggled. "I suppose they think that makes him less liable to cause trouble. We don't have many men on the staff for perhaps quite obvious reasons. Lastly there is Ned. He does the odd jobs the caretaker can't manage and tends our vegetable garden. He is a little simple."

Maud paused and gave Annie a long look.

"Now, why are you here, my girl?"

Annie was ready for such a question.

"I work for Miss Clara Fitzgerald. She is currently incapacitated and has asked me to conduct some discreet enquiries for her."

"What sort of enquiries?"

"You may have noted the rumours concerning Mr Graves in the newspapers?"

Maud raised an eyebrow.

"That I have."

"Well, Miss Fitzgerald has been asked to find the source of these rumours and put them to rest. The family are naturally very distressed by them," Annie elaborated on the truth a little.

"I don't doubt it. But why come here?"

"Truth be told, so far there are very few clues in this matter, and Miss Fitzgerald thought perhaps talking to others who knew Mr Graves might lead to some ideas."

"He was a patron here," Maud agreed. "Would you like my honest opinion of him?"

"Yes," Annie said.

Maud sat a little more upright in her chair, her humour had evaporated. She looked stern, though still jovial.

"He was like every other man who comes here," Maud began. "They think they are being philanthropic, but as soon as they are among the girls their minds wander. They imagine what those girls must have done. It is dreadful, you can see it crossing their minds. It is bad enough when the girls have to go back out into the real world, but in here this is supposed to be a safe haven. I don't have much time for men."

Annie could tell that. She recalled that Maud had always been suspicious of the male species, even at the munitions factory she had viewed the few men who worked among the girls with a mixture of distaste and fear.

"Aside from that," Annie tried to delve deeper, "what did you make of Mr Graves?"

"He was hard working," Maud grudgingly admitted. "And he was very interested in education. He helped appoint our teachers. He also helped with the legal affairs of the school. I can't fault him for that."

"Did he strike you as troubled?"

"Tired, more like. He worked all the hours God sent. I told him once that the Sabbath was a day of rest and he merely smiled and nodded. I always assumed he worked himself into the grave."

"Perhaps he did," Annie nodded, feeling she was getting nowhere. "He certainly didn't seem to have any enemies."

"Oh, I wouldn't say that," a twinkle returned to Maud's eyes. "Mr Graves had principles, and a man with principles tends to collect enemies. He didn't like people who avoided paying their taxes for a start. He said that was unfair on the poor. He was very conscientious on the subject, but I know he almost came to blows with Mr Vanburgh when the latter avoided paying the full death duties on his late father's estate."

"That is interesting," Annie perked up. "Who is Mr Vanburgh?"

"He is on the committee for the Brighton Pavilion, but he is also a very wealthy man. His father made a fortune in overseas plantations. Mr Vanburgh lives on that fortune. You may recall he provided a float for the carnival last year?"

Annie admitted she didn't.

"It was on the theme of Jonah and the Whale. It was rather crass. Mr Vanburgh played Jonah, and everyone said his 'whale' was the cruel tongue of public opinion. He doesn't exactly make friends."

"But to come to blows with Mr Graves must have been quite serious?"

"I think Mr Graves had talked about taking legal action against him. Mr Vanburgh did not like that at all. It was just before Mr Graves became seriously ill at Christmas. I think his health prevented him pursuing the action."

"Though perhaps he contemplated trying again once he was recovered?"

"Perhaps."

"Maud, is there anything else useful you can think to tell me about Mr Graves?"

Maud pursed her lips as she thought about the question. She had not spent a great deal of time with the late solicitor for personal reasons. She was uncomfortable alone in the company of men and let Mrs Dobbs deal with any queries Mr Graves had had.

"I recall..." she hesitated. "Have you met the Graves family?"

"Yes," Annie said. "Not exactly mourning their loss, I might add."

"Except for Julia Graves?"

Annie tilted her head.

"Now that you mention it, she did seem distressed. The only one, in fact, who seemed to truly mourn him."

"Would it surprise you if I said Julia Graves was once an inmate here?"

It did surprise Annie. In fact, it astounded her. She shook her head.

"Julia Graves?"

"It was before my time here," Maud added. "I suppose it must be thirty years ago. It is rather a sorry saga and I only know the end of it. I am in charge of the records here, you see, and I was sorting them one day and came across her name. I read the file, but it was only brief. It seems Julia Graves had a baby."

Annie was stunned.

"Should you be telling me this?"

"No," Maud admitted. "But I think you ought to know, seeing as how there are rumours around Mr Graves' death. It was after she was sent here that he became a patron. It is unusual for a girl from a decent family to be sent here, you know. Typically it is hushed up. But I think her father was rather a tyrant and wanted to shame her."

"Was she here long?"

"About six months."

"And the baby?"

"The records didn't say."

Annie was flustered. She was trying to imagine the woman she had seen grieving at the Graves' house, sitting in a place such as this. It was almost impossible to imagine Julia Graves as anything but a respectable woman. Almost. There had been something odd there, something Annie could not put her finger on. She had to get back and report this to Clara.

"Thank you for your time, Maud."

Maud gave a shrug, as if to say it was nothing.

"Why not call again Thursday evening," she said as she escorted Annie to the door. "We have a guest speaker coming to talk about women's war work. Many of the women here were otherwise engaged during the conflict and did no honest work. You could share your experiences."

Annie thought not. The last thing she wanted to do was talk about the war. But she gave Maud a 'perhaps' and then fled as fast as she could. She had to reveal these new insights to Clara. Were they important? Perhaps, perhaps not, but it seemed there was a lot more in the Graves family's past than anyone cared to let on.

Chapter Eleven

Mr Hatton owned a charabanc touring company. It was a gentile sort of business, not overly taxing on the nerves or the mind. Arranging someone's weekend away to Cornwall or Southend-on-Sea was not particularly challenging, once you had the number of passengers and their names written down. Unfortunately, Mr Hatton was not a man who suited genteel work. It left his busy and slightly over-imaginative mind free to dwell on other circumstances; such as why his wife suddenly seemed so friendly with that Duncan Platt who they had met at a neighbour's Christmas party. Mr Hatton spent a lot of time thinking and very rarely did his thoughts stray onto wise topics, instead he fretted. He fretted while he organised peoples' random trips away. He fretted while working out the petrol expenses for the charabancs. He fretted while contacting hotels and bed and breakfasts and placing bookings for the more luxurious excursions. He fretted every minute of every day, then he came home and argued with his wife over the imagined ills he had dreamed she was doing against him while at his desk.

Had he owned a more cerebral business, one that occupied his thoughts and made a use of his natural ability to see problems ahead of time, then perhaps his marriage would not now be in a state of decline. Perhaps his wife would not be preparing to leave him and secretly drawing up divorce papers. Perhaps he would not be sitting in front of Clara Fitzgerald feeling like a common criminal. Mr Hatton shifted uncomfortably in his chair. It was his lunch break and he had agreed to nip out from the office to see Miss Fitzgerald to discuss the possibility of arranging a special charabanc tour which could be offered as a prize at the next Brighton Pavilion fundraiser. It was a ploy, naturally, but she had to get Mr Hatton out of his office somehow. She had explained to him why she could not come to him and he had duly agreed to go to her. However, he had not long been in Miss Fitzgerald's parlour, before he realised he had been lured away on a ruse.

"I apologise for the deception," Clara told him as she poured a large cup of tea for her guest. "Sugar?"

Mr Hatton gave a nod.

"Three, please."

Clara measured out three teaspoons, mildly surprised at Mr Hatton's sweet tooth. Most people had long ago given up on sugar in their tea due to shortages during the war. Mr Hatton was clearly not one of them. She passed over the cup, noting that he probably needed the sugar, he looked in a state of shock and she had yet to tell him why he had been asked there. He had the appearance of a man with a guilty conscience.

"As I said when you entered, I need to discuss a rather personal matter. Had I been able I would have come to your office. As it is I had to ask you here under false pretences, though," Clara paused to muse, "I have wondered about taking a charabanc tour. Do the drivers go very fast?"

"We prefer them to keep to a respectable twenty miles per hour at the most," Mr Hatton briefly went back into his business self. "Our charabancs have never had an accident."

"That is most reassuring," Clara agreed. "I quite fancy

a trip."

"I can recommend our Lake District tour. It is one of the longer ones, but you stop each day at a notable landmark or beauty spot, and we can arrange all the hotel details. It is rather nice in the summer."

"I shall think about it," Clara changed the subject. "But back to the reason I brought you here. I have been asked to investigate a few curious inconsistencies that have arisen from the sudden passing of Mr Graves."

"Poor man," Mr Hatton said in a rather rushed tone.

"Did you know him?"

"No," Mr Hatton admitted. "But I arranged a weekend tour for his mother and sisters a couple of years ago."

"Were you aware that your wife was one of his clients?"

Mr Hatton gulped down a particularly large mouthful of tea. His eyes bulged a little as he trembled on the verge of choking himself, then he swallowed again and the moment passed.

"No," he said in a very small voice.

Clara looked at him rather sternly. She didn't like being lied to, especially by such a poor liar. Mr Hatton shifted in his chair again, and gave a little cough.

"Shortly after Mr Graves' death it was discovered that certain legal documents had gone missing from his desk. They were, in fact, the very last papers he was working on. Now, a full search of his office has not revealed these missing documents. As you may imagine his partner, Mr Erikson, is most perturbed by the matter. I fear you will be most perturbed too, for the papers were related to your wife."

Mr Hatton managed to raise his teacup to his mouth and take another gulp.

"Truly?" he said, almost feigning an expression of complete surprise. "My wife had not mentioned anything? Ah, Mr Graves was a specialist in wills, I imagine she was just updating hers."

"Mr Hatton, must we play such silly games? Surely

you understand the reason I asked you here?"

"I'm afraid you have me at a loss," Mr Hatton put his teacup back in its saucer and balanced it precariously on the arm of his chair. "My wife does not tell me everything she does."

Clara gave a sigh. This was becoming tedious.

"Mr Hatton, since you won't allow me to do this delicately, I must be blunt. I know that you have the divorce papers that your wife was having drawn up by Mr Graves."

The teacup went crashing to the floor and smashed. Clara looked at the mess with an expression of resignation. She was glad she had not brought out her mother's china.

"I rather liked that cup."

"I… I apologise. My elbow… twitched. I..." Mr Hatton looked down forlornly at the fragments of porcelain on the floor. "I will replace it."

"Mr Hatton, a teacup is really not important. But, please, do stop lying to me. I have spoken with your wife. It was quite by chance, in fact, because I was asked to investigate the last moments of Mr Graves' life and your wife happened to be his last appointment. It was while I was talking with her that I discovered papers were missing. Now, there are very few people who would be interested in stealing such documents. I can't help but find myself thinking that you have the most to gain from removing those papers from Mr Graves' desk."

Mr Hatton jumped. It was a natural reaction and told Clara more than the denial that followed.

"I have never been in Mr Graves' office!"

"You were not in his office between eleven o'clock and midday?"

"No!"

"But you do have the divorce papers?"

Mr Hatton grimaced.

"I don't know what you are talking about," he insisted unconvincingly.

Clara decided it was time to be tough.

"Mr Hatton, this matter comes down to two things, you either explain to me how you came to have hold of the divorce documents drawn up for your wife, or I have to assume you took them from Mr Graves' office personally. Now, that means that either you were the last person to see Mr Graves alive, and that you possibly killed him, or you entered his office after he was dead and took an opportunity to steal your wife's papers. Personally, I would rather be facing the lesser charge of stealing, than the charge of murder."

"Murder!" Mr Hatton jumped up from his chair and looked as though he was going to bolt for the door.

"Stay put, Mr Hatton! I have not gone to the police yet, but if you leave without explaining yourself I shall be forced to present this matter to them!"

Mr Hatton hesitated between flight or remaining to talk with Clara. He was like a terrified hare that has heard the bay of hounds, but can't decide which direction the danger is coming from. In the end he reluctantly sat down, deciding he would rather plead his case to Clara than to a policeman. Besides, it would be much more humiliating to have to tell another man that his wife was intending to divorce him.

"I didn't kill Mr Graves. I thought he died of natural causes?"

"There is a question mark over that matter as well."

"I was telling the truth when I said I had never been in Mr Graves' office," Mr Hatton desperately hoped Clara would believe him. "I did not even know my wife had gone to see him until last week."

"What happened last week?" Clara asked.

"I had a telephone call, at my office," Mr Hatton straightened his tie unconsciously, his mouth had gone dreadfully dry. "I don't know who the caller was, other than it was a woman's voice. She said, 'was I aware that my wife was planning to divorce me?' I laughed at the idea, but the caller said she had the papers to prove it.

Taken from Mr Graves' desk. I swear I did not know that they were taken on the day he died!"

Clara reluctantly believed him.

"What did the caller want?"

"What else? Money," Mr Hatton sank into himself miserably. "She would post me the documents if I sent her fifty pounds. That is a lot of money, Miss Fitzgerald, especially for documents I had never even seen. I said to the caller, how could I know they were genuine? She said she would send me the top page of the papers, while keeping the remainder. Then I would see they were real."

"And did she?"

"Yes. It arrived the next day in a brown envelope. I read the name and my heart sank," Mr Hatton actually gave a sniff, and Clara dreaded he was about to cry. "I never imagined… I could have tolerated anything but that. Why would Susan do such a thing to me?"

Clara motioned that that was one question she could not answer.

"Once I saw the document was genuine I was scared. There was a notation on the corner of the paper that indicated it was the first of five pages. What did the other four pages contain, I asked myself," Mr Hatton trembled. "I didn't know what to do and then the telephone went again and it was the same caller. She wanted to know if I had received the post yet. I had to say yes. She explained her terms to me again. Fifty pounds for the remaining four pages which she would post to me, or she would make the documents public to my friends and colleagues. I suppose I am too proud, Miss Fitzgerald, but I couldn't face that happening."

"You agreed to pay her?"

"Yes. I took the money out in cash. It stripped all my savings…" Mr Hatton bit his lip. "I had to leave the cash in an envelope at Mrs Dill's bakery. Apparently she would know why I was leaving it. Then I just had to wait for the documents to arrive. Thank heavens the caller was honest enough to send me the papers."

"And once you had them, you threatened your wife?"

"Yes," Mr Hatton twiddled his thumbs. "I'm not particularly proud of that."

"Nor should you be," Clara sighed. "You can't blackmail a person into loving you. Mr Hatton, if you wish to save your marriage it is about time you started listening to your wife. Perhaps it is already too late, perhaps not. You both have lost faith in each other. It would not be a bad idea to restart your relationship by burning those divorce papers. Consider it an act of reconciliation."

Mr Hatton said nothing. He was thinking of the fifty pounds he had just paid for papers that may be little better than kindling.

"Did you recognise the voice of the caller?" Clara asked, trying to be helpful at least.

"No, well..." Mr Hatton stopped himself and began to think more clearly about the voice on the 'phone. "You see, I almost imagined that I did recognise it."

"Who did you suppose it might be?"

Mr Hatton had to give this some thought. He tapped his lip with his finger.

"It rang a bell," he said. "I thought it was one of my better customers. I do speak to a lot of people, but not everyone is on the 'phone. Yes, it struck me that I knew that voice."

"But you can't put a name to it?" Clara pressed.

Mr Hatton screwed up his eyes to think.

"I had the impression, when I was listening to the voice, that I had arranged a coach trip for them. And the place that sprang to mind was Dorset. I remember people best when I link them with places they have been to on our charabancs. Yes, it was an out-of-season booking because it was cheaper. I remember picturing Dorset in the depths of autumn when I listened to the voice."

"Does that help?" Clara asked, a tad bemused.

"Who did I arrange an autumn trip to Dorset for?" Mr Hatton tapped his lip again, "Dr Moody went on one, but that was not his voice. Nor was it one of the Clatton sisters. I speak with them quite often."

Clara did not usually like to lead her witnesses, but this was one situation when a hint might prove useful.

"I don't suppose," she said carefully, "it was one of the Graves family?"

Mr Hatton actually went pale. He looked at her aghast.

"Why, yes. It could just be. But..." Mr Hatton shook his head. "What would that mean?"

"Oh, it could mean many things," Clara suggested vaguely, not wishing to mention that the obvious answer was that it meant one of the Graves family had been snooping around Mr Graves' office shortly after his death. It may even mean that one of them was responsible for his untimely demise.

"It could just have been old Mrs Graves," Mr Hatton concluded. "Now you say the name I should have noticed it before. She has quite a distinctive voice."

The clock chimed the hour and Mr Hatton suddenly sprang from his chair.

"My dinner hour is over!"

"Thank you for your time, Mr Hatton. Good luck with your wife. I won't mention your receiving stolen goods to the police unless it becomes absolutely necessary," Clara called out behind him as he raced for the door. He left so fast he almost forgot his hat.

Clara remained in her chair and thought over the matter. Whichever way you looked at it, all avenues took her back to the Graves family. But could old Mrs Graves be a master forger? And, even if she was, why forge a will to leave everything to one of her daughters, rather than to herself? It was all very odd, and somehow Clara would have to get out of the house and visit that family. She looked miserably at her foot. That was easier said than done.

Chapter Twelve

Annie had taken to the detective lark as a favour to Clara. She had insisted it was not 'her cup of tea', but after a few days acting as Clara's agent, she was beginning to get swept up by the investigative spirit, so much so, in fact, that she was about to do something unimaginable a few days before – she was going to 'follow up a lead' without consulting Clara first. It was rather exciting. Annie wasn't the sort of person to make snap decisions. She liked to contemplate the outcomes of her actions carefully. But when she had left the Ladies' House of Reform an impulse had come over her to follow up something Maud had said. It seemed such a good idea, that Annie quite forgot she was supposed to be getting soap powder flakes and that she had left Tommy in charge of a leg of mutton, which was no doubt burning to a cinder that very moment. She just couldn't resist the detecting urge. So this was why Clara was so often late for dinner!

Annie stormed across the road in the direction of the Post Office. She needed an address, and the best place to find that was in the Post Office Directory. Mrs Jenkins, the postmistress, glanced up at her as she entered.

"No parcels today, Annie," she called out, but Annie failed to hear her. She was on a case and nothing else mattered.

Annie thumbed through the pages of the directory to the section marked 'V'. There were a surprising number of names, but it wasn't hard to scroll down the page and spot Vanburgh. Annie noted the address, then marched out again. Mr Vanburgh was the first person she had heard of who did not like Mr Graves. She doubted he was a killer, but he might just be able to give an insight into the solicitor who allegedly had no enemies. When you speak to a recently deceased person's friends, you very rarely hear anything negative about them. It goes against the grain to speak ill of the dead. But, a deceased person's enemies are another matter. Very often the death of their adversary leaves them feeling freer to voice their own opinion on them. Annie felt this was a very logical conclusion and something worthy of Clara. Mr Vanburgh might just be the lead she was looking for.

As it turned out, Mr Vanburgh also lived along Old Steine. His house was one of the few that had a car parked outside; a navy blue and black sporty thing that glistened in the sunlight. He was a playboy who spent most of his time inventing new ways to spend his vast fortune. He was unmarried and seemed inclined to stay that way. Though, according to local gossip, he had more than one mistress to provide him with feminine company when he desired it.

As Annie approached his house her nerve started to go a little. Now her eager plans, that had at first seemed so logical, suddenly seemed less sound. She hesitated on the pavement. Perhaps it was not too late to turn around and walk home. Instead of arriving unannounced, Annie would ask Clara to ring ahead and make an appointment for her, if she felt Mr Vanburgh was a viable witness that is. Annie was on the verge of leaving when the front door burst open and Mr Vanburgh, in full driving gear, marched down the front steps to his car. He paused on the last step because Annie was standing right in front of him. He lifted up his driving goggles.

"Well, hello," he grinned.

Annie blushed before she could help herself. She had to say something.

"I am here on behalf of Miss Clara Fitzgerald," she said, flustered.

"The private detective?" Vanburgh raised an eyebrow. "She was run over by a hearse."

"Yes. That's why I am acting on her behalf."

"And why are you on my doorstep?" Mr Vanburgh was grinning from ear to ear, assessing the girl before him.

She was quite clearly a servant of some description, but her clothes were neat and pretty new. She had reddened hands from scrubby and washing, but her shoes were smartly polished and her hat had a new ribbon.

"It's about Mr Graves," Annie blurted out.

Mr Vanburgh gave her an enquiring look.

"What about Mr Graves?" he asked.

"There have been some complications," Annie answered. "Miss Fitzgerald has been asked to make some discreet enquiries."

"But naturally that is difficult while she is housebound?"

"Naturally."

Mr Vanburgh gave a nod of understanding.

"Jump in the car then."

Annie started.

"Pardon me?"

"I am going for a drive, so if you wish to talk with me you will have to come along," Mr Vanburgh headed for his car clearly assuming Annie would follow.

Annie hesitated. She had heard what could happen to a girl who went for a ride in a motor car, it was a regular feature of the stories which she could in her weekly magazines. Men seemed to lose their heads in cars. Annie did what she had done throughout this investigation and imagined what Clara would do. Clara disliked motor cars, but she would not let that distract her from a case in hand. If Mr Vanburgh wanted to talk while driving, so be it.

Annie walked to the car and accepted Mr Vanburgh's proffered hand to help her up and in. The car was taller than she had imagined and, once in the seat, she felt strangely elevated. Before her was a big dashboard covered with shiny dials, and an impressively large steering wheel thrust out in front of the driver's seat. Vanburgh went to the front of the car and turned the starting handle. After a couple of cranks the engine rumbled into life. Annie gave another start as she heard the engine roaring all around her.

Vanburgh got into the driver's seat and away they went, heading down Old Steine and out towards the countryside.

"So, you want to ask about Mr Graves?" Vanburgh said loudly, so as to be heard over the rumbling engine.

Annie was clinging to her hat so it didn't fly off.

"I have been calling on all of those people who knew Mr Graves, to gather information," she managed to say.

"That could take some time!"

"Rather," Annie allowed herself a small sigh. "You see, I have been trying to form a picture of Mr Graves outside of the one his family and the popular press present."

"You want to know about the real man?"

"Yes. But everyone is so decently polite about him that it is proving quite challenging. And then your name was mentioned..."

"And you thought his arch enemy might be a better bet for a true picture of the man?"

Annie considered that question, wondering what was the right response.

"If you want the truth... yes."

Vanburgh laughed. It was a jolly sound and he had clearly not taken offence.

"I can truly help you there, because I disliked the man. Probably I am the only soul in Brighton who did."

"Why?"

"Graves was a buffoon, a principled one, no doubt, but a buffoon nonetheless. We fell out over a number of things. In fact, we hardly ever seemed able to see eye-to-eye."

"You were involved in the same committees?"

"Some. But Mr Graves was of the opinion that I was not worthy to be a part of such causes. To him I was a playboy with too much money and time on my hands."

Annie considered this. She knew what Clara would ask next, but she was not brave enough to do the same. So she skirted the matter.

"What did you think of Mr Graves?"

"He was pompous, controlling. Believed he, and only he, knew what was best for this town. I have no doubt he did a lot of good work, but I found him hugely irritating."

"Did he have any enemies?"

"Aside from myself?" Mr Vanburgh laughed again. "Perhaps. All men have some enemies. Are you suggesting his death was something other than natural?"

"I'm not suggesting anything," Annie said hastily.

They had left Brighton behind and were now driving into the countryside. All around them there was nothing but fields. Annie started to feel a long way from home.

"Graves disapproved of my lifestyle. Can I help that I was left a lot of money by my father?" Vanburgh paused for an answer. Annie obliged.

"I suppose not."

"Precisely. It was my good fortune to have a wealthy father. I intend to enjoy that fortune, why not? All anybody wants in this life is enough money to enjoy themselves and be carefree. I was lucky enough to be handed that on a plate. Graves begrudged me the fact," Vanburgh pulled the car up onto a grass verge and stopped the engine. "I like this view. Grass and cows as far as the eye can see, and not a person in sight."

Annie, a hardened townie despite her parents having a smallholding, gazed at the scene around her with something akin to despair.

"If you want to know the truth about Graves, you should look to his family," Vanburgh continued, stretching one arm along the back of the car seat. Annie eyed the movement suspiciously.

"I already have. They don't appear interested in talking about him. Actually, it is hard to feel they are grieved by his loss at all."

"Even Julia Graves?"

Annie glanced at Vanburgh. There was a sly look in his eye.

"What do you know about Julia?"

"Oh, come, come. We all hear gossip. I know that Mr Graves thought a lot of his sister Julia. Perhaps, out of them all, she was the only one he felt true affection for. His mother, after all, was a leech, and his other sisters were little better."

"That is quite a harsh comment."

"Is it?" Vanburgh gazed out at the fields. "Tell me, if Mr Graves had not had so many hangers-on to support, would he have worked himself into the ground?"

Annie had no answer for that. It was true the Graves family had lived beyond their means for many years, to the extent that Mr Graves had needed to heavily supplement his mother's and sisters' incomes. Perhaps that created resentment, it was difficult to say. But then, wasn't Julia part of that same family?

"Quite frankly, if you were looking for a murderer I would go no further than the women in Mr Graves' life," Vanburgh leaned towards Annie and spoke in a low, conspiratorial tone.

She glanced at him out of the corner of her eye, but made no other sign that she had noticed his proximity.

"I have been reading all the speculation in the papers," Vanburgh continued, his voice almost a whisper. "I am hardly surprised that Miss Fitzgerald has become involved. But now, this is far too pleasant a morning to be discussing such dark things."

Mr Vanburgh was getting altogether too close for

comfort. Annie tried to remember how to open the car door.

"Do you know, I don't think I caught your name," Vanburgh's arm slipped around Annie's shoulder, he leaned towards her and she could feel his breath on her cheek. Enough was enough.

"Mr Vanburgh, if you do not move away this instant I shall scream loud enough for the whole of Brighton to hear, no matter how many miles away the town is," Annie took Vanburgh's arm and firmly removed it from her shoulder. "I have an investigation to attend to. Please drive me back to town."

Vanburgh eyed her, a look of devious delight glinting in his eyes. He was still weighing up the possibility of pushing his luck.

"Mr Vanburgh!" Annie said sternly, in the voice she had once used to cow the teenage boys in the Sunday School class she taught. "If you are unable to drive, I shall walk home!"

Vanburgh gave a groan and saw he was not going to win. He flopped back into his seat. He was not the sort to disgrace a lady's honour without her consent. He conceded defeat. After a moment he hopped out of the car and turned the starting handle. Annie relaxed a little as he returned to the driver's side and carefully turned the car around.

"Do you have a fellow?" Vanburgh asked as they slipped back into the lane.

"I do indeed," Annie said firmly.

Vanburgh nodded.

"Lucky man," he grinned at her.

Annie was mortified to discover she was blushing again.

"You can tell Miss Fitzgerald, if she has further questions, I am quite happy to pay her a call," Vanburgh continued, back to business. "I would quite like to meet a female private detective. Though, I hope she doesn't think I had anything to do with Graves' death?"

"The idea has not come up," Annie assured him. "Though, I fear there may be some truth to the speculation that he was murdered."

"But how?" Vanburgh asked. "The coroner found nothing."

"So it would seem. Really, it is quite confusing," Annie shrugged. "Someone may have entered his office after his last client had left. In fact, it seems very likely someone did."

"But you can't say who?"

"No."

Vanburgh concentrated on taking a rather tight corner before speaking again.

"Graves was not the sort of man to attract dangerous enemies. He didn't get close enough to people. That is why his acquaintances only have vague things to say about him. Aside from Mr Erikson, his business partner, he had no true friends. His life was his work, I recognised that. Even as his enemy I can't say I hated him. You could only really dislike Mr Graves. But I sensed there was always something else, something buried beneath the surface. Dig into his family and I think you will find the key to this tragedy."

"On that I think you may be right."

Annie was glad to see the houses of Brighton ahead of them. Already her sense of unease was evaporating.

"I suppose my mutton joint is burnt beyond recognition," she said aloud without thinking.

Mr Vanburgh grinned at her.

"I could offer you dinner?" he suggested.

"You are very determined, Mr Vanburgh."

"I like a challenge."

"On this occasion I am afraid I must decline."

Vanburgh pulled up to the pavement.

"Perhaps Miss Fitzgerald will dine with me sometime?"

Annie hopped out of the car as swiftly as she could.

"I shall pass the message along. Thank you for your

time."

Mr Vanburgh laughed.

"Any time, my dear, any time!"

Then he swept off in his flashy sports car.

Chapter Thirteen

Clara had questions; how had someone snuck into the offices of Erikson and Graves without being seen? How long would it take them to get in, kill Graves and get out again? How well would the perpetrator need to know the building? None of these questions could be answered by Mr Erikson himself, after all, he had never attempted to sneak in and out of his own building. Clara needed to know 'how' a crime could have been committed before she could decide 'if' there had actually been one. There was nothing else for it but to rope in her friends and attempt to recreate the crime. Clara would be the overseer of this experiment, point-blank refusing to remain stuck at home, unable to see for herself the results of this venture. She would act the part of Graves sitting in his office, that way she might get a better idea of what his last moments were like. Erikson was briefed on the plan and agreed that Sunday afternoon would be suitable for the procedure. Clara called in the services of Oliver Bankes, local photographer and friend, and ex-military doctor Colonel Brandt, who had a good rational mind. The arrangements all made, Clara went to bed on Saturday feeling that she was at last doing something productive.

The offices of Erikson and Graves did not open on the

Sabbath. It therefore came as something of a surprise to the returning churchgoers and casual Sunday passers-by, to see through the front window a young man sitting behind the secretary's desk. They were even more disconcerted when the said young man gave them a jolly wave and a smile. Poor Mr Erikson, trying to enjoy his one afternoon off, found himself inundated by phone calls and worried clients on his doorstep, all utterly convinced his offices were in the process of being burgled. Having explained that everything was perfectly all right to more than a dozen individuals, Mr Erikson gave up on his restful afternoon and trundled down to his offices. Once inside, he placed himself prominently in the front window, to make it plain to the curious of Brighton that Mr Erikson was fully aware there were people in his offices on a Sunday. In any case, it gave him the opportunity to hear first-hand what Clara had discovered in her series of experiments.

The man behind the desk, who had waved so gleefully at shocked bystanders was, of course, Tommy. Confined to the ground floor by his infuriating wheelchair, he had stepped into the place usually filled by Mr Erikson's secretary. Clara, meanwhile, had insisted on limping up the stairs to Mr Graves' office, where she was in prime position to observe the entire operation. It also gave her the opportunity to speculate on what Mr Graves might have last seen or heard on his final fateful day.

Oliver Bankes was to play the part of the murderer. He had a photography shop in the high street and his skills with a camera often came in useful in Clara's cases. In fact, he had been in his shop when the unfortunate Mr Graves had been found dead, and could recall the sight of the ambulance coming to fetch the body and the huge crowd of gawkers who had hovered around the office. Oliver had considered taking a picture of the curious scene, but decided it was rather improper under the circumstances. Just like everyone else in Brighton, he had heard the recent rumours that Mr Graves' death was something other than natural, but until Clara had found him in his shop that very morning, he had considered them all a load of nonsense. As a man also dedicated to his work, (after all, he was in his shop on a Sunday, though he was not open to the public) he could imagine how Mr Graves drove himself to an early funeral. Sometimes he feared that would be his lot too, especially after a long week when all his body ached from weariness and he could not remember the last time he had eaten a decent meal. To hear that Graves may have been murdered from Clara, who did not bandy around such topics lightly, had quite stunned him.

As for Colonel Brandt, little stunned him. His days as a medical student, followed by a stint in the army, had taught him that nothing was too extraordinary. He had seen men die in very peculiar fashions, sometimes quite inexplicably. He recalled one Sergeant-Major who had seen action in the Boer War. He seemed hard-as-nails. He had come close to losing a leg and had taken a bullet to the shoulder without letting it shake his nerve. Then one day he was bitten by a snake. The offending creature was killed by his own revolver and proved to be a non-poisonous variety. Despite this, the Sergeant-Major was dead within the hour. He had a mortal fear of snakes, and the only conclusion that anyone could come to about his unexpected death, was that he was so convinced the snake bite was fatal he willed himself to a premature end. Certainly the wound was completely harmless. Brandt, therefore, could well imagine a man working himself to death. He was yet to be persuaded anyone had murdered Mr Graves. He chose to go by the coroner's findings, being a fellow medical man. There was nothing suspicious about the body, therefore it seemed unlikely there was anything suspicious about the death.

Despite his reservations, Brandt had willingly agreed to help Clara. The alternative was to sit in his club all afternoon, which was rather a depressing place to be on a Sunday at the best of times. Too many old unmarried men together in one place resulted in a rather maudlin atmosphere.

The only person missing from the party was Annie, who had refused to leave her Sunday roast to attend the experiment. She had spent all week salvaging meals from the burnt offerings Tommy and Clara produced, and she was not going to let her roast go the same way. They would thank her later when her perfectly cooked beef joint was presented to them.

Annie's refusal did leave a slight dilemma; Clara was working on the theory that all her main suspects were female, thus, if they came over the back wall and through the yard door to kill Mr Graves in secret, they had to have done so wearing a skirt. Had she been fit and able, Clara would have been scaling the back wall to see how challenging it was and also how long it took. However, she was not able, so the job had to fall to Oliver and, as he immediately refused to wear a skirt for the experiment, she would have to factor that complication in later.

Oliver was sent outside to await a signal to begin. Clara theorised that whoever clambered in through the back yard had done so shortly after the departure of Mrs Hatton. They were probably completely familiar with Mr Graves' routine, and knew that his secretary was careful to book his last appointment of the morning for no later than 10.30. Equally, they would probably know that Mr Erikson took his partner out to lunch at noon. That left a window of around an hour for the affair to be dealt with. Since only a fool would cut such limited time fine, Clara assumed that the assailant would have watched for Mrs Hatton to leave, then would have slipped into the offices and attacked Mr Graves. With all this in mind, Clara informed Oliver that he was to linger discreetly across the road and, when Tommy opened and closed the front door, he was to pause a moment longer and then head behind the building to make his secret entrance. Most importantly, he was not to draw attention to himself.

As it turned out there was a small bakery across the

road from the solicitors' office, which had a pair of tables in the window where customers could sit and partake of a pot of tea if they wished. It was closed on a Sunday, but Oliver decided that it would be the perfect place for someone to watch the offices of Erikson and Graves without appearing suspicious. So he hovered in front of the large bakery window, kicking his heels and trying to seem innocuous, until Tommy opened and closed the front door. Then Oliver walked across the road in a casual fashion; following Clara's instruction not to draw attention to his actions he walked in a diagonal path so that he could not be seen from the window of the solicitors' office. He paused for a moment outside a shoemaker's shop. There was an alley running down beside the offices. Oliver waited a second, as if perusing the window display of the shoemaker's, then he headed down the alley.

Nearly at the bottom of the alley he came to a gate, which he assumed led into the back yard of Erikson and Graves. He tried it out of curiosity, but it was soundly locked. His only option now was the wall. Someone had been kind enough to stack some old wooden crates against it and he used these as improvised steps to give himself a head start. Once he had his hands on the top of the wall it was simply a case of hoisting himself up and then dropping down the other side. It only took him a few moments and he was in the yard.

Brushing brick dust from his trousers he headed for the back door of the building. Mr Erikson had said that during the day the door was usually not locked. Oliver tried the handle and the door swung inwards. He held his breath a moment in case the door gave out a condemning creak, but it was very well oiled and it made no sound as he entered. He didn't close the door properly, but let it rest on the latch, then he glanced down the corridor. The hallway that ran between the front room and the back of the house was parallel with the side wall. Looking down it Oliver had a clear view of the main door to the building, and anyone entering at that moment would have seen him, but he could not see the spot where Tommy was sitting. Nor could Tommy see him. This convenient blind spot meant that Oliver could approach the stairs without fear of being caught. He took the steps gingerly, they were uncarpeted and he dare not take them too fast in case someone heard his footsteps. As it happened, he was only up the first three treads when the fourth groaned under his weight loudly enough to wake the dead.

Almost at once Tommy and Mr Erikson appeared behind him, while Colonel Brandt appeared from Mr Erikson's office and Clara hobbled out from Mr Graves'.

"Try again, Oliver. From the stairs," Clara instructed.

Everyone returned to their places. Oliver mounted the stairs again, being careful to avoid the fourth step, he had nearly reached the top when he put his foot on the ninth step and it let out a groan even louder than the previous one. Yet again four faces immediately appeared.

"Once more, Oliver."

Oliver started over for the second time. This time he dodged step number four and number nine, he was certain he would now make it to Mr Graves' office without anyone noticing. He placed a toe on the landing and it let out a squeak. With a small groan Oliver watched the faces reappear.

"I won't make you do it again," Clara said, leaning heavily on a walking stick in the doorway of Mr Graves' room. "It has proved the point I was interested in anyway. Whoever entered this building knew it well and knew which stairs to avoid to make no sound. How long did Oliver take, Colonel?"

Colonel Brandt had been timing Oliver's escapade with his brass pocket watch.

"Around nine minutes, taking off a couple due to redoing the staircase."

"That puts the time our murderer could have arrived in Mr Graves' office at around eleven o'clock. Assuming they started off the moment Mrs Hatton left," Clara hobbled back into the office and lowered herself into Mr Graves' chair with a sigh. "Now, they entered the office quietly. Mr Erikson didn't hear anything but the door moving, so I think we should assume Mr Graves knew who had entered, else he would have demanded to know why they were there and likely caused more fuss. So here they are in the room. Oliver, stand before the desk."

Oliver obeyed.

"So here is Mr Graves," Clara motioned to herself. "He sees the intruder but doesn't react loudly. Perhaps they talk for a few moments, then something happens and Mr Graves dies."

Clara looked around her as if a clue would suddenly spring into view and explain the mystery.

"We have no murder weapon. All we can say for certain was that it was quiet."

"Perhaps the intruder upset Mr Graves so much he had a heart attack?" Brandt suggested.

"In that case we would have to assume they argued, but there is no evidence for that. Unless you mean the intruder's appearance was so shocking to Mr Graves he died of fright?"

"But we have already established the intruder was familiar with the building," Oliver interrupted. "That implies they knew Mr Graves well. The sight of them walking into a room would surely not be shocking?"

"No, I still think this was more than just an accident," Clara glanced at the desk. "Had Mr Graves died unexpectedly before the intruder appeared then, more than likely, they would have been shocked themselves and fled hastily. People who don't intend to murder someone do not usually remain calm when that person drops dead before them. No, this person was so unmoved by Mr Graves' demise that they spent time searching the office while his corpse was growing cold. They stole papers which they thought they could make money out of. Not the actions of someone in shock, I don't think. The intruder came with the intention of killing Graves.

Everything points to that, including the underhand fashion in which they entered the building. But we are still left with that unanswerable question – how?"

There were no answers that the room could offer up to Clara. She had proved to her satisfaction that it was possible for a person familiar with the building to reach Mr Graves unnoticed, but she still had no clue as to the method used to murder him. For that matter it was just possible, as Brandt postulated, that his death was accidental.

"This is really a conundrum," Brandt said sympathetically. "The coroner offered no insights?"

"No. Everything seemed in order," Clara sighed. "I am really bothered about all this. How can someone kill a man and leave no trace?"

Clara glanced around once more and her eyes lingered on the water glass and jug sitting on a sideboard near the door. She remembered how Erikson had mentioned that Mr Graves was rather particular about having glasses of water near his papers. Yet the glass had been found on his desk. Coincidence or mishap? Had the murderer drunk from the glass and left it on the desk in error? There were too many variables. In truth Clara felt no further forward and she had no better answers for Mr Erikson than she did an hour ago. If there was something in this room to hint at what had become of Mr Graves, she could not see it. There was a key to this mystery somewhere, she just had to find it.

"I think we have done what we can for today," she said at last. "Thank you both for your help, would you like to come back to the house for dinner?"

Neither man was inclined to pass up a chance to enjoy one of Annie's roasts. Clara took a last look around the office before she accepted Oliver's help to limp down the stairs. Oh Mr Graves, she called out silently to the ether, if only you could give me a clue! But, as she had learned in her very first case, the dead were rather uninterested in the affairs of the living, and she was on her own if she wanted to bring Mr Graves' killer to justice.

Chapter Fourteen

Monday morning dawned and Clara found herself regretting the previous day's adventures. Her foot was extremely sore and just hobbling downstairs was agony. Her plan to head to the police station and examine the files (if there were any) on the death of Mr Graves senior had to be curtailed. Instead Tommy offered to go to the library and look through the old newspapers for any information. Clara appreciated his assistance, but couldn't help but feel glum; she was not used to being so housebound.

Annie did not stand for self-pity, she felt it was unproductive. So when she brought through a cup of tea and toast for Clara' breakfast she swiftly confronted the problem head-on.

"Young lady, cheer yourself up!" she instructed firmly.

Clara glowered at her a little.

"So you can't leave the house. I'm sure with a mind like yours you can think up some means for occupying yourself indoors," Annie continued, completely undeterred.

"I need to visit the Graves family," Clara answered miserably.

"I can do that. My kitchen is clean, we have plenty of

cold meat left over for dinner, so no need to put you in charge of an oven, thank goodness," Annie stood before Clara, hands on hips, looking formidable. "I'll take Tommy to the library, then catch the tram to the outskirts and see the Graves women again. You want me to probe about the suspect will?"

"Well, yes. That and the mysterious death of Mr Graves' father. I don't believe two men can die in exactly the same manner by coincidence."

"I shall head out at once," Annie said stoutly. "Now, what will you do while I am out?"

Clara really didn't know. All the things she wanted to do were outside of the house.

"Perhaps it is time you placed your concerns before Inspector Park-Coombs?" Tommy suggested. "See if he can spare you the time for a visit."

Clara conceded it was about time she briefed the Inspector on the situation. Better he be warned of the situation then to suddenly descend on him with a murder case, if there was one, of course. Clara still had to face the possibility that Mr Graves' death was accidental, or even a pure coincidence. But someone had stolen papers from his office, and though she had promised Mr Hatton to keep his name out of the matter, she did need to inform the police of the strange goings-on at the solicitors' office.

"There is one other person I wish to speak to," Clara suddenly had an idea. "Annie, would you be so kind as to drop in to the offices of Mr Erikson and ask his secretary to call on me at her earliest convenience."

"Say no more, it is done," Annie promised.

With everyone's goals for the morning decided upon, they went their separate ways, each determined to find the final clue that would unravel the Graves mystery.

~~~*~~~

Tommy was a regular presence in the library and tended to get special treatment from the female assistants who viewed him as some sort of wounded war hero. It was one of the rare occasions, when they fawned over him and asked him what he was looking for today, that Tommy did not resent his disabilities. Tommy was quite often to be found surrounded by old piles of the Brighton Gazette, surveying them for some nugget of information. The ladies knew this and, almost as soon as he appeared, they were asking him which year he wished to see issues from? For once Tommy could not give them a direct answer. Instead they had to search the card catalogue that indexed the articles in the paper for anything referring to Mr Graves senior. Fortunately, the death of such a prominent figure in Brighton society attracted a great deal of press coverage.

Before long Tommy was happily ensconced behind a pile of papers from the year 1899. He picked up the issue the index had listed as containing Mr Graves' obituary.

"On November 6th last, local solicitor and well-loved Brighton figure, Mr Zachary Graves, was found deceased in his place of business. It is with much sorrow that the town bids farewell to this notable figure, who donated so much of his time to charitable causes.

"Mr Graves moved to Brighton in 1875 and opened a small solicitor's office. It was in this same office, 24 years later, that he was sadly found deceased earlier this month. Mr Graves was well-remembered for his support for the poor and vulnerable, often giving his time freely to those who could not afford his usual fees. He is fondly remembered for defending the ten factory workers who went on strike in 1889 due to a reduction in wages. The men were taken to court by their employer, where Mr Graves deftly defended their right to industrial action and a reasonable, living wage. The success of his defence has forever earned him a place in the minds of workers in the town.

"Mr Graves was in the fifty-seventh year of his life. His untimely death, which has shocked many, has been attributed to excessive work and lack of relaxation. It is well known Mr Graves was a man rarely seen out of his office and who attended as many committee meetings and functions as his busy diary allowed. It is thought his tragic early death was speeded by a bout of bronchial fever and the lack of a warm fire in his office. Mr Graves refused to light a fire before December 1st, declaring that if the poor must abide the cold, so should he.

"Zachary Graves leaves behind a wife and six children. His son runs a solicitor's office of his own in the town and has stated the property will be in mourning through the winter and black drapes have already appeared at the windows. Mr Graves' funeral will be held on the 14th of this month and a large turn-out of mourners is anticipated."

Tommy put the paper down and mused on the information he had just read. Mr Graves senior had died in the exact same fashion as his son. Not only had his death been blamed on over-work, but a bronchial infection was suspected as speeding his demise. He might as well have been reading the obituary of his son, 22 years later. Tommy opened the next issue of the paper and found himself staring at a picture of Zachary Graves. The man looked a typical Victorian gent, with side-whiskers and a stern glare. He did not seem the sort who would take care of the poor, at least not in a charitable fashion. Tommy found himself studying the grainy picture, trying to find an insight into this peculiar man.

"Excuse me?"

Tommy glanced up and saw that there was an elderly man standing at his shoulder. The man was clearly of working stock, his jacket was rather worn and he was holding his cloth cap in his hands. Years of working outdoors in all weathers had prematurely aged his face and made judging his precise age difficult, but he was clearly into his twilight years.

"Excuse me, but I couldn't help over-hearing you talking to the librarians. You are curious about Mr Zachary Graves?"

"I am," Tommy said.

The old man ran the cap through his hands.

"Could I ask, why?"

Tommy gave him a gentle smile.

"Professional curiosity," he said. "You must have heard the rumours concerning his son's death?"

"I have indeed," the old man looked troubled. "Is there any truth in them?"

"That is what I am trying to find out. I am working on behalf of the family, but please don't tell anyone."

The old man took this all very seriously and looked utterly downhearted by the news. After another moment of clear indecision, he pulled out the chair next to Tommy's at the reading table and sat down.

"I was very sorry to hear about the death of Mr Graves. Two deaths like that in a family is a tragedy. I said to myself, it just can't be right."

"It does seem extremely curious," Tommy nodded.

"I said there was something odd about it when I first heard," the old man finally placed his cap on the table. "My name is Robert Ewan. I used to do the gardens for the Graves family, until I retired to go live with my daughter, that is."

"You must have known the family quite well then?"

"As best a man can when he works for someone," Mr Ewan nodded. "There is always a barrier between employer and the man he employs. Can't be helped."

"Were you working for them when Mr Graves senior died?"

"Yes. That was a terrible winter," Mr Ewan shook his head sadly. "It was such a shock. I remember I was raking leaves when the Graves' cook came out and told me. Said the family were in an awful state, as can be imagined."

"Was there ever any thought that Zachary Graves may have died of something other than natural causes?"

Mr Ewan paused and stared at the paper before Tommy. The page with Mr Graves' grainy picture was still lying open and Mr Ewan's eyes seemed to focus on his long dead employer.

"Nothing was ever said to me. Mr Graves had been quite ill the month before. Everyone said he should have taken more time away from his work, but he refused. He never would have a fire lit in his office or the house before December 1st, you know."

"Yes, it mentioned that in the paper."

"I suppose it also spoke of him as a very worthy and charitable soul?"

"Yes," Tommy met Mr Ewan's eyes. "Was that not so?"

"It all depended on who you were," Mr Ewan plucked an invisible grain of dirt from his cap. "I never had any complaints. Always had good tools to hand and a new jacket every Christmas. I used to say, 'Mr Graves, there is no call for giving me another new jacket, this here one is fine.' But he did insist, said I could save them for when I retired. Well, that I did and this is one of them," Robert Ewan tapped his jacket. "In that sense, he was kind as kind could be. But he was hard on his family. Never could quite work out why, but sometimes I swear his daughters were wearing worse dresses than their maids. And he never seemed to do anything but shout at his wife. Sometimes I reckoned they were all rather glad he spent so much time at the office."

"Aside from his family, did he have disagreements with anyone else?"

"There were those he won cases against. Powerful people sometimes. All dead now, though," Mr Ewan seemed to reflect on the past. "I never suspected he was murdered though."

"Until his son's rather coincidental death?"

"Yes."

Both men were silent for a lengthy moment.

"I always thought..." Mr Ewan hesitated. He glanced around himself to see who was nearby. The library was fairly empty and no one was near to over-hear his comments. "I always thought that if anyone was going to do in Mr Graves it would be his family."

"Do you mean Zachary?"

"Yes. As I say he treated his family badly. All that talk in the papers about his philanthropy, I remember reading it at the time, he was a man loved by strangers, but detested by his family."

"Those are strong words, Mr Ewan."

"But truth, nonetheless. That youngest girl, Julia, she went wild under the strain. She got herself into trouble and he turned her out of the house and sent her to that reform school for ladies of the night. I ask you, what sort of father does a thing like that? She may have lost her head, but she was never one of those sort," Mr Ewan looked quite distressed by the matter.

"What of his relationship with his son?"

"It was little better than the one he had with the girls. They were quite similar in many ways and the son worked his heart out to earn his father's approval. But it never came. You would imagine, after all, that Zachary Graves would have taken his son into his business, but no. He insisted the lad make his own way, like he had done. That being said the younger Mr Graves did a darn sight better for himself than the father."

"What about the Graves women, Mr Ewan? What can you tell me about them?"

Mr Ewan shrugged.

"I didn't see them so much. It was a lovely garden they had, but they hardly ever came into it. Saying that, nor did Mr Graves. Now, I will say that the widow, that would be Emily Graves, she was a fine looking lady in her day. She had poise and grace. I truly wondered some days why she had married her husband who was rather stern and a trifle uncomfortable next to her beauty. I think he wanted to keep her shut away from the world, for fear she would find someone else who appreciated her grandeur better than him.

"If I recall rightly she was the youngest daughter of a country squire. Didn't have much money of her own, mind, so perhaps that was why she pinned her hopes to an up-and-coming solicitor. Perhaps Zachary Graves was more dashing in his younger days. Time can wither us all," Mr Ewan held up his weather-worn hands.

"But the marriage soured?"

"Some do," Mr Ewan shrugged. "You live long enough you see the most promising of matches end in dislike, boredom and even hatred. One day it is all ringing bells in church, the next people are yelling at each other and finding ways to hurt the person they supposedly vowed to cherish 'til death do part. Sometimes they even decide to hasten that bit."

"Unfortunately, that is true," Tommy had seen quite a few cases where a marriage had ended in disaster, if not a suspicious death. "What of the Graves' girls?"

"I hardly saw them," Mr Ewan answered. "They kept themselves in the house. They never went to parties or out for strolls like most young ladies do. I don't ever recall there being a suitor at the house. Perhaps their father wouldn't allow it."

"Perhaps not," Tommy felt he had learned a lot more from the fortuitous meeting with Mr Ewan than from the papers. He took one last glance at the stern façade of Zachary Graves staring out from the newsprint.

"Thank you for stopping to speak with me, Mr Ewan."

"That's all right, sir. I just don't like the idea of someone going around harming members of the same family. That isn't the way civilised people should behave."

"No, I suppose not."

Mr Ewan stood and retrieved his cap.

"Mind you," Mr Ewan paused. "I could quite understand why the Graves women might want to do it."

With that mysterious remark Mr Ewan wandered off.

Chapter Fifteen

Inspector Park-Coombs was very good about making tea for the invalided Clara. He insisted, in fact. He had even been good enough to stop on his way from the station and buy a small packet of shortbread biscuits. Having heard about Clara's misfortune, he was certain she was going out of her mind stuck in the house and a packet of biscuits was the least he could do to try and ease her troubles. He had also taken the liberty of smuggling some files out of the police station for her. He knew what would cheer Clara up.

"The files on the first Mr Graves' death," he handed over a cardboard folder.

"How did you know I was on the case?"

"My dear Clara, as soon as I heard the rumours flying about town I knew you would be rooting around trying to solve the mystery."

Clara looked abashed that she was so easy to predict. Park-Coombs wavered.

"In any case, Mr Erikson came to my office to report the loss of some papers, believing them stolen, and he rather spilled the beans on your involvement."

"I had asked him to keep the matter out of police hands while I tried to find the papers," Clara was a little disgruntled to hear Erikson had gone behind her back.

"He is a solicitor," Park-Coombs shrugged. "Has to do everything by the book. Do you know who took the papers?"

"I have a good hunch, but I have promised certain people to keep the matter discreet."

"Understood. I really don't have the manpower to go chasing down lost paperwork, more serious crimes have my attention."

"Anything interesting at the moment?"

Park-Coombs eased himself more comfortably into his chair and gave a sigh of contentment.

"Squire Hawkins has had his pack of hounds pinched. We know who did it, a local farmer who has his own pack and who has been arguing with the squire for years now over whose dogs should be used in the local hunt. Quite frankly it's a right pickle. I go to look at these dogs, well they look all the same to me, how am I to say if they were the ones stolen from Hawkins? Naturally the farmer claims he bought in a new lot recently. We will be picking this one apart for weeks."

"Oh dear. But are you investigating any real crimes?"

"Someone has been robbing the post boxes around Hove. We suspect an opportunist looking for money sent with letters and cards. And we have the usual round of fights, drunks and casual criminals to keep our eyes on."

"Anyone reported a lost dog?"

"No. Why?"

"Never mind," Clara was thinking of a certain small poodle that appeared to have decided it was now living in the Fitzgerald residence on a permanent basis. She had found it on her bed that morning when she awoke.

"I did have a look into the hearse mystery."

Clara perked up.

"The horse was sabotaged," she said

"Yes. It has quite distressed the undertakers. They keep telling me they have a reputation to uphold. I suspect Mrs Graves, the widow, that is. She placed some flowers on the hearse just before it set off. Special request, apparently. Seemed odd to me, considering the notice in the paper had advised people to not send flowers."

"Mr Graves had an aversion to them," Clara agreed.

"Mrs Graves has denied tampering with the horse, naturally."

"Do you have a motive in mind?"

"Oh, delayed rage at her late husband, perhaps? He was not the most attentive of spouses."

Clara stared at her bandaged foot thoughtfully.

"I propose another reason. I think Mrs Graves suspects, like the rest of us, that her husband's death was less than natural. Perhaps she sabotaged the horse to deliberately cause a commotion and keep Mr Graves' untimely death fresh in peoples' minds. A runaway hearse tends to be talked about for a long time, much longer than the ordinary funeral of even a notable man such as Mr Graves. Could it be she was trying to draw attention to the matter?"

"Well, she did that," Park-Coombs motioned to Clara's foot. "For better or worse, everyone is talking about Mr Graves."

"So, Inspector, as you are already aware that I am investigating the circumstances of Mr Graves' death, perhaps I ought to bring you up to speed with the matter?"

"That would be appreciated."

"Let us begin with the reasons some suspect Mr Graves' death as being unnatural. Firstly, but perhaps most significantly, his demise bears an uncanny resemblance to the death of his father some twenty years past."

"Hence bringing you the files," Park-Coombs nodded. "Mr Erikson hinted that there might be a link between the two deaths. Before my time as an inspector, mind you."

"1899, to be precise," Clara glanced at the papers the Inspector had brought her. "We shall return to them in a moment. Second, Mr Erikson believes he heard someone entering Mr Graves' office after his last client had left the building. The identity of this visitor remains a mystery, but, more than likely, they were present when Mr Graves died."

"Erikson didn't tell me that," Park-Coombs grumbled.

"I think he feels rather embarrassed to reveal what he heard. He wonders if he really heard anything at all. I believe he did. I have run a few experiments…"

"On Sunday, yes. Do you know how many 'concerned' citizens I had at the station that day? Your name is mud with the Desk Sergeant."

Clara's relationship with the Desk Sergeant was hardly of the best to begin with, so she shrugged off this revelation.

"In any case, my experiments demonstrated that it was completely feasible for someone to slip into the offices of Erikson and Graves via the back door and confront Mr Graves unnoticed by anyone else. However, they would need to know the property to avoid some extremely creaky stairs that would have given them away."

"Equally, had a stranger gone into Mr Graves' office he likely would have caused a fuss."

"Unless he was already dead. That is a possibility I cannot rule out just yet. It is unlikely as the time between the last client leaving and Mr Erikson hearing a door open and close is extremely short. But it can't be ignored."

"You know that Dr Deàth found nothing suspicious about the case?"

"Yes, I have spoken to him and I respect his abilities."

"But?"

Clara hesitated. How could she explain this gut feeling she had that something sinister had happened to Mr Graves, something the good coroner had missed, or which, more probably, left so little sign as to make the death seem natural. Inspector Park-Coombs chose to fill the silence.

"You are a little too young to remember, but back when I was being trained as a policeman, there was still a lot of talk about how arsenic could be used as the perfect murder weapon. You see, arsenic poisoning mimics the symptoms of Cholera or, for that matter, any particularly acute stomach ailment. It was very hard, before the doctors figured out a way to find even the most minute traces of arsenic in a person, to prove someone had been murdered that way. I daresay many escaped the noose for that reason alone. Death by arsenic was perceived as the perfect murder for a time."

"Are you suggesting we may be looking for a poisonous substance yet to be commonly known to science, as the cause for Mr Graves' death?"

"That sounds like a plot of a Penny Dreadful, no, I don't quite mean that. Just, that certain suspicious deaths can look entirely innocent."

"Someone was in that office after Graves was dead. The missing papers are proof enough. Mr Erikson had no reason to hide those papers, and had he done so he would not have reported them missing to you."

"No," Park-Coombs concurred.

"Oh, if only I knew what went on in that office between 11 o'clock and 12 o'clock!" Clara gave out a groan.

"I don't think the files on Mr Graves senior will be very enlightening," the Inspector admitted bluntly. "Skimming through them it seemed no one suspected the death was anything but natural. He was found slumped at his desk, a glass of water by his hand…"

"A glass of water?" Clara quickly flicked open the file she had been handed and scanned the papers inside. "Just like Mr Graves junior, another link if ever I saw it!"

"The glass? Many people have glasses of water on their desk. I do, for instance."

"Yes, but Mr Graves was particular about having water near his paperwork. The glass on his desk was odd. Out-of-place. The sort of thing that makes you pause.

Unusual things at a sudden death always draw my attention."

"Are you suggesting there was something in the water?"

Was that what Clara was suggesting?

"Even if there was it is too late to know now, far, far too late. Oh!" Clara glowered at her foot again. "I feel so utterly useless sitting here. I have leads I cannot follow, clues I cannot chase down. There is something here! But knowing what it is eludes me!"

Park-Coombs remained silent. Finally Clara looked at him.

"It is time we treated this as a full-scale case of murder," she fixed her gaze on him. "I think we will have to exhume the body."

"To find what?"

"Something. Something that explains all this madness."

"Exhumations are a lot of paperwork. I will have to apply to my superiors and get permission from the family. Without evidence that the man was murdered I can't do anything without the Graves' approval."

"And I doubt they will give it," Clara understood. "Then we must scour Dr Deàth's original report for a hint. There has to be something in it. No one dies so innocuously as all that!"

Park-Coombs rested his hands on his knees, deeply considering the situation.

"Do you have a motive?"

"Only that Mr Graves' last will appears to be a forgery leaving all his money to a single sister."

"Money," the Inspector sighed. "How many murders have I investigated where that was the cause? Too many. So the single sister kills her brother to prevent her fraud being identified and so she can inherit all his money?"

"Only, that particular sister, I have it on good authority, was extremely distressed by her brother's death. The only member of the family, indeed, to be affected in such a way."

"Was a guilty conscience mistaken for distress?"

Clara could not deny that as a possibility, though she felt Annie was capable of discriminating between the two. Annie had been emphatic about the genuine grief she saw in Julia's face and demeanour.

"Can you offer me any other motive?" Clara asked after a pause. "You must hear things as a policeman. Are the Graves as upstanding as they appear to be?"

"I have had no complaints about Mr Graves or the family," Park-Coombs said. "Though the youngest girl, Julia, has had a few near scrapes with the law. She is troubled. I suppose that is the best way to put it."

"How so?"

"I think a doctor would call her a hysteric. She suddenly flies off the handle. I have a small, but extremely interesting file on her, though, as she is still alive, bringing that from the station for you to look at would have been a serious breach of regulations."

"Understood. But can you explain a little more about the things she does?"

"Nothing that has raised much alarm. Her name has been kept discreetly out of the papers. I think the last time I was called to a situation with her, she was refusing to leave one of the public parks so the park-keeper could lock the gates. She wouldn't talk to anyone. Just sat on a bench glaring out at the duck pond. She appeared to not know we were even present. I had to call out a doctor. Eventually we were able to move her."

"So far she doesn't sound violent?"

"She threw paint at a local vicar. That was a couple of years back. He had preached a rather volatile sermon on the sins of the flesh and the shame of illegitimacy. I doubt she was alone in wanting to lash out. The matter was resolved very quietly and no charges were made."

"Knowing Julia's history, I can understand her reaction," Clara said softly.

"Interestingly enough, I have also had cause to visit

the late Mr Graves on a rather serious matter."

Clara almost started.

"Really?"

"Yes, one of the ladies at the House of Reform insisted he had made unwelcome advances to her. I'm afraid few took her seriously. With women like that it is very difficult and Mr Graves was a very good patron."

"I see the problem," Clara sighed, it was always the same story. The vulnerable were penalised for being vulnerable. "In your opinion, was she telling the truth?"

Park-Coombs took a long while to reply.

"It was all very odd. We had never had a complaint before and Mr Graves was not a man we considered... of that nature. He was a family man, someone who was always very proper."

"But was she telling the truth?"

Again there was a long hesitation.

"You know, I think she was. Except, I don't think the advances he made to her were quite what she imagined."

Now Clara was truly curious.

"How so?"

"He wanted to talk to her alone and to know her name. He asked about her family and her age. It was all talk. She perceived this as an attempt to win her trust and to lead to something more intimate. Ladies who have only experienced that side of men tend to suspect us of all having only one thing in mind."

"But you think it was something else?"

"He was questioning her for some reason. Not because he wanted to seduce her. Rather, I think he wanted to know more about her."

"But why?"

"You tell me."

Clara considered the evidence at length, then she glanced up.

"Julia Graves was sent to the House of Reform because she fell pregnant. What, I wonder, became of the child?"

"Did Mr Graves see a family resemblance, perhaps?

Did he link ages and dates and draw certain conclusions? What irony, a child born in the House of Reform returning some years later to avail herself of its services."

"Who was this woman, Inspector?"

Park-Coombs scratched at his chin.

"I don't recall her name, but I could find it. Whether you will be able to trace her is another matter."

"That is for me to decide. We might be utterly wrong and he spoke with her for reasons we have not even guessed at."

"It all comes back to that family, doesn't it," the Inspector nodded solemnly. "Tread carefully, Clara."

"I always do, but a man is dead and I cannot ignore that fact."

"Nor can I. But I think you will be digging through a lot of dirt to find the truth."

"So be it," Clara said, though not lightly. "The truth cannot be hidden forever."

The Inspector gave her a look as if to say he wasn't so sure about that.

Chapter Sixteen

Annie rapped on the door of the Graves' family home. She was confident someone would be about, as the family were not renowned for socialising. In fact, they were almost recluses, except for the late Mr Graves. A maid answered the door and took her request to see the family. A short while later she was standing in the parlour surrounded by Mrs Graves and three of her daughters – Julia was absent from the gathering.

"Good morning, Miss Green. Quite unexpected to see you again. Are you still working on behalf of Miss Fitzgerald?" enquired Mrs Graves.

"Yes," Annie confirmed.

"And how is her foot?"

"Healing a little too slowly for her liking. Clara is a dreadful patient," Annie realised her slip of formality as she spoke and became flustered.

Mrs Graves merely smiled.

"Please send Clara my condolences. I take it you are more friend than agent to her?"

Annie blushed.

"We've known each other since the war. She saved my life and I repay her kindness as best I can."

"So, I take it she has sent you on this errand for a

reason?"

Annie hesitated. This was the moment she had been dreading. Should she be blunt, or should she hedge around the topic of the suspicious will?

"Clara has unearthed some new information concerning your son's death," Annie decided to be cautious. "She thought you ought to be informed."

"That is most kind," Mrs Graves seemed to deflate. "I take it she believes she has proof he was murdered?"

"His death is troubling," Annie said vaguely. "A number of things do not add up. There is evidence that someone entered his office via the back door after Mr Graves' last client had left. Someone he knew."

All the women before Annie now looked worried. Annie tried to surreptitiously glance at their faces to see if one of them looked guilty. She found she could not tell, they all just looked deeply upset.

"Mr Graves' death may have been accidental," she tried to ease the blow. "We have not ruled that out. However, someone was in that office either just before or just after he died, and stole certain papers from his desk."

Mrs Graves seemed to cough a little.

"Is that so?" she said.

"These papers have been used for the purposes of extortion, which I am told is a very serious matter. Along with that disturbing information, we are now concerned that Mr Graves' last will is not all it appears to be."

Abruptly Annabel Graves perked up.

"You mean it is a fake? I said as much!" she looked triumphantly at her sisters. "I knew Isaac would not be so cruel as to leave us penniless!"

"You were never penniless, dear. Your father's investments are quite sufficient to see us all out in comfort," Mrs Graves interrupted.

"Your version of comfort and my version are extremely different," Annabel said sourly. "In any case, I never could fathom why Isaac would want to leave all his money to Julia. It doesn't make any sense."

"He was always fond of Julia," Christiana Graves interjected. She was staring wistfully out the window, as if thinking of what she might do with the money she would inherit.

"But to disown his wife like that?" Annabel persisted. "What has she ever done to deserve such brutality? Poor woman would be left destitute, she only had Isaac and her aging mother after all."

"Perhaps Miss Green could explain why the will is in question?" Mrs Graves said very firmly, taking charge before a real argument broke out. "Well, Miss Green?"

"A handwriting expert has examined the will and raised suspicions about its authorship. Also it differs considerably from the last will Mr Erikson saw his partner make," Annie explained.

"A handwriting expert!" Annabel clapped her hands. "Well that surely seals the fact!"

"Was our brother killed because of this fake will?" Agatha Graves suddenly asked.

"You mean the forger became impatient?" Annabel was quite excited now. "I do believe you could have a point, Agatha. The forger may have been fearful of discovery."

But how did they do it?" Agatha continued.

They all looked to Annie.

"That is something we are still to determine," Annie decided to push her luck. "Did none of you ever think it curious that your father passed in a similar fashion to your brother?"

Annie looked to the three sisters, who all took on blank expressions.

"Daddy died in his office," Christiana shrugged. "I suppose it was a little odd Isaac did the same, but they both worked all the hours God sent."

"My husband was a dedicated solicitor, Miss Green. Very dedicated," Mrs Graves added. "He put himself out for people and that was his undoing. There never a question that he was murdered. I believe the inquest ruled it was heart failure brought on by acute exhaustion. My husband only took Sunday afternoons off, you know. It was only a matter of time before his body felt the strain."

"Isaac was just the same," Annabel agreed. "Why, I don't suppose he remembered the last time he took a whole weekend off! That was why Mr Erikson always insisted on taking him out for lunch daily."

"You knew about the arrangement?"

"Oh yes, we all did. It had gone on for years."

"Who would want to kill daddy?" Christiana Graves raised the awkward question. "Yes, he could be rather a grump sometimes and he was mean with money, but he was not particularly awful."

"People don't have to be awful to be murdered, dear," Annabel said. "Why, I was reading only the other day of a poor woman who was murdered because her relatives wanted to sell her house and make some money. I doubt she was particularly awful."

"Unlucky, more like," Agatha nodded. "She should have made a will stating the relatives would not inherit the house."

"I imagine she was ignorant of their intentions."

"Girls! Can we stop discussing such an awful subject!" Mrs Graves suddenly looked very frail sitting in her chair. She had sunk in on herself as she listened to her daughters gossip about murder. "Why would anyone want to murder my dear Isaac?"

Mrs Graves produced a handkerchief from her sleeve and dabbed at her eyes.

"He was a good man, Miss Green, no one can deny that."

Annie nodded.

"So I heard. He helped people."

"Yes, he was always a very kind soul. Even as a boy. I shall always remember him as a little five-year-old at a garden party serving cake to our elderly guests. He was always so polite and helpful. A delightful son. I was very proud of him," tears had begun to trickle down Mrs

Graves' face. "I will never forgive the person who stole him from me."

"I am sorry to have caused you such distress," Annie said with genuine regret. "But you needed to be informed."

She glanced at the women, but sensed she would get no further information and none of them were about to admit to forging Isaac Graves' will. Annie decided it was time to depart. She made her excuses, feeling deeply unhappy that she had caused Mrs Graves such grief, then fled the house as swiftly as she dared. She feared she had done little more than upset the Graves family that morning, certainly she felt she had not learned anything new. She was deep in thought as she walked out of the garden into the lane and almost collided with Julia Graves. The girl looked at her like a startled rabbit, then relaxed when she recognised her face.

"Oh, Miss Green. For one awful moment I thought you were a press reporter. For the most part they have left us be, but every now and again we find one lurking about the garden."

"They are a nuisance," Annie concurred, without really knowing if that was true. "I was just paying a call on your family to explain where matters stand concerning your brother's death."

"Is there a problem?" Julia looked surprised.

"There are concerns your brother's death was not natural," Annie clarified.

Julia looked duly shocked. She began to tremble and had to perch herself against the garden wall.

"I always thought one of them would do him in," she said stiffly.

Annie was curious.

"Them?"

"My sisters. Not my mother, no, she cherished Isaac. But one of them!"

Annie was slightly stunned by the revelation, not least because of the outright fury and hate that now surged onto Julia's face.

"They wanted his money. That is all they care about. Isaac worked himself into the ground for them, but did they care? No, they were always take, take, take."

"And what of you?" Annie asked gently. "Were you not shocked when Mr Graves' will stated that he had left all his money to you?"

"I was very shocked!" Julia snapped. "I never expected such consideration, though I was the only one of his sisters who had shown him any affection. I shouldn't blame them entirely, I suppose. They are mere products of our father's upbringing. He made money the centre of our world by depriving us of it. In my case I learned that money does not bring happiness, but my sisters learned to gather money in any way they could. By fair or foul means."

"But, to suggest murder?"

"Why do you seem so surprised? Surely most people are killed by their families, very often over money," Julia was bitter. She folded her arms across her chest and hunched over. "Fair or foul means, that is how they behave."

"Perhaps you will be relieved to know there are doubts about your brother's last will? It may be a forgery."

Julia didn't move.

"I didn't forge it."

"I never said you did."

"But it looks that way because I get all the money," Julia was glum. "I would much rather Isaac was alive, you know."

"I believe you. But if forgery is the case, who else would be inclined to create such a will?"

Julia shook her head.

"You see? It looks like I did it. But I didn't. Not that anyone will believe that. Will the police become involved? They will think I did it. I shan't hold my breath that they will imagine me innocent for an instant."

Annie found Julia's bluntness distressing, especially as

she already seemed resigned to being found guilty. Annie feared that Julia would barely even protest if the police arrested her and charged her with the death of her brother, and since she seemed the only one of the Graves family who was mourning Isaac's passing, that was most distressing.

"You mustn't give in so easily," Annie told her.

Julia looked up at her in surprise. Perhaps it was the first time anyone had suggested she should do anything aside from resigning herself to her fate.

"How did they kill him?" Julia asked.

"We don't know. That remains a mystery. But we know someone was in his office when he should have been alone. Someone who knew the layout of the building very well, down to which steps creaked on the staircase."

"That rules me out," Julia almost smiled. "I have never been to the offices. Never been inclined. I don't like legal stuff."

Julia gave a shudder to emphasis her feelings.

"That is a very good start," Annie said. "Now, Julia, is there anything you can tell me that might be useful to solving this riddle?"

"I can't think of anything," Julia shook her head.

"You knew your brother well, yes?"

"Yes."

"Did he ever keep a glass of water on his desk?"

"Oh no!" Julia looked horrified. "He would not allow it unless it somehow spilled on important papers!"

"That's what Clara thought and what Mr Erikson told us. I am glad you can confirm it."

"Why do you ask?" Julia was now curious rather than miserable.

"There was a glass of water on Mr Graves' desk when he was found dead. It seemed out of place from the start, but we can't fathom the reason for it."

Julia stood upright, pushing herself away from the wall.

"It shouldn't have been there!"

"No," Annie agreed. "But it was."

Julia rubbed at her temple absently with one hand. She was trying to piece all this information together and find the truth.

"Do you suppose there is a link between your brother's death and that of your father?" Annie probed.

"That was a very long time ago," Julia said. "I took little notice."

"I understand your relations with your father were not of the best."

Julia glared at Annie. Her look was so sharp it almost made Annie take a step back.

"Who said so?"

"I paid a call on the Ladies' House of Reform…"

Julia began to shake with suppressed fury.

"What a delightful visit that must have been for you," she said. "I suppose they could not wait to reveal my sorry tale?"

"It came up as part of the conversation. I was there to draw background information on your brother, to see if I could account for his murder through one of his charitable causes…"

"Spare me your excuses. You are no better than the rest. Only interested in gossip!" Julia looked fit to lash out.

Annie suddenly doubted her previous assessment that the woman was incapable of murder.

"It was not a judgement," Annie tried to appease her. "I simply meant that I could understand you not being interested in your father's death."

"My relationship with my father is none of your affair," Julia's voice was low and fierce. "I suggest you focus on my brother's death and leave the past where it belongs."

"Only if the past bears no relation on the present," Annie didn't like to be intimidated, she had had enough of people getting cross with her just because she was trying to help. "If you can assure me your past has no bearing on your brother's murder, then I shall leave it alone."

"Why should it?" Julia snapped.

"Because secrets have a tendency to fester over time."

"My past has nothing to do with my brother's death!" Julia turned her back on Annie and stormed towards the house.

Annie watched her go. She wasn't sure she entirely believed her, there was the mystery of the will for a start. Did someone alter it to favour Julia as compensation for a past wrong? If that was not the case, then why would anyone (aside from Julia herself) want to alter the will in such a way? Annie sensed there was something here she was not seeing. It was time to regroup and present Clara with this new information. One thing Annie was sure of – any one of the Graves family could have murdered the unfortunate Isaac. Even the one person who seemed to love him the most.

Chapter Seventeen

Clara went very carefully through the file on Zachary Graves that Inspector Park-Coombs had left with her. There was nothing that particularly struck her as significant, in truth the file was rather flimsy. Zachary had gone to work one morning as usual, there was no sign that he was ill or that he might not return. He saw clients between 10am and 2pm. No one reported that he showed any indication of being unwell. He seemed his usual businesslike self. Zachary Graves spent the afternoon catching up on paperwork, or at least that is what his secretary imagined. He had no appointments arranged, so she had no reason to go to his office and see him until just before leaving off at 5pm. She was in for a shock. Zachary Graves was slumped over his desk, a flurry of papers cast before him and onto the floor. In one hand a pen was still clutched. Next to the other was a glass of water. The unfortunate secretary thought he had been taken ill and rushed to the nearest doctor. When he returned with her and examined Zachary, it was plain to see he had been dead for some time.

The inquest ruled that Zachary Graves had died of natural causes, heart failure was suggested, certainly there seemed no evidence of anything more suspicious. A post-mortem had been performed, though it had been rather simplistic. There was no sign of disease about the body, just the throat appeared somewhat inflamed. This was explained away by a recent cold the late Mr Graves had suffered. The coroner was satisfied that Zachary Graves had quite simply, and naturally, passed away.

Clara pushed the file away and mulled over the information. There was no hint of foul play in the case of Zachary's demise, but then nor had there been in the case of Isaac's, until coincidences started to be noticed between the two sudden deaths. What was to be made of it all? And then there was that glass of water – both men had one by their hand as they died. It would be interesting to know if Zachary felt the same about water glasses on his desk as his son did. Suspicious glasses made Clara imagine poison, but it was too late in both cases to discover if that had been the case. The glass from Isaac Graves' desk would have been cleaned and used a dozen times over since his death, and who knew where the one from Zachary's office had ended up?

There had to be a link. Two related men dying in exactly the same fashion, albeit more than twenty years apart, jangled at Clara's nerves. But it also implied the same killer. What would trigger a person to kill one man and then to kill his son in the exact same fashion twenty years later?

She was distracted from her thoughts by the doorbell. Waiting on her doorstep was Miss Dorothy Parker. Dot, to her friends. Dot was in her late twenties, a robust creature who had resigned herself to a working career rather than to one of marriage and family. She had been in the employ of Erikson and Graves for the last five years, having replaced their previous elderly secretary. Dot believed she had dramatically improved the everyday running of the offices in that time. She prided herself on her cataloguing systems and her efficient paperwork. People dying at their desks impacted on this efficiency and bothered her a great deal. She was unsettled, especially because people (namely press people) kept asking her questions about the late Mr Graves, implying that someone had murdered him. Dot felt this reflected rather badly on her. She suspected people were hinting that she had neglected her duty by allowing a wanton killer to enter the offices. Dot was a good gatekeeper and the thought that someone had snuck past her caused her considerable pain.

When Clara had asked her to visit and have a chat, she had almost declined. Yet another person with questions over her efficiency and ability, she thought. But then she had paused to think – perhaps it was time she gave her side of the story? Perhaps it was time Dot explained why this was not her fault? Clara might be the ideal person to hear Dot's woes. After all, she was not connected with the press, nor was she related to Mr Graves. She was as close to an unbiased listener as Dot could get. After some soul-searching, Dot had decided she really did need to talk to someone, and it might as well be Clara.

"This will be entirely confidential?" Dot asked as she was shown into the parlour.

She baulked at the sight of Bramble flopped in the armchair reserved for guests. He gave her a look that implied she would be well advised to sit elsewhere. Clara shooed him off.

"Yes, entirely confidential," Clara paused. "You don't know anyone who has lost a dog, do you?"

Dot shook her head.

"Filthy things," she declared.

Bramble looked hurt. Clara found herself offended too, much to her surprise.

"I find many dogs cleaner than people," she observed. "But each to their own."

She made a point of putting Dot in the chair Bramble had just vacated. Dot sat primly on the edge.

"Now, I asked you over just to clarify a few details about the sad demise of Mr Graves. Do you mind discussing it?"

"No. But I want to assure you it was not my fault."

Clara looked at Dot curiously.

"Not your fault?" she said.

"I know what everyone is thinking, that I have failed to keep the offices shipshape. That is simply not the case! I work very hard Miss Fitzgerald, very hard! If someone sneaked in without my knowing it was not for want of effort!" Dot seemed to perch even further forward on the chair. "I made every effort. Who would have thought someone would climb the wall and come in by the back door? I lock it now. If only I had thought of it sooner…"

"I hardly think you can blame yourself," Clara tried to appease her. "You were not to know."

"I should have heard them," Dot looked most unhappy. "I really can't fathom it. In all my years at the offices I have never let someone in without knowing who they were and whether they were expected. I am very good at that, Miss Fitzgerald, nobody gets past me unless I say so."

Clara could well imagine.

"You have been with Mr Erikson these last five years?"

"Yes, I took over from Maud Jones upon her retirement. I don't like to speak ill of people, but she had let the offices run down terribly. The filing system was a complete shambles. How Mr Erikson and Mr Graves managed I can hardly say. It took me weeks to put things in order. More to the point, she used to let people visit the office without an appointment! I had endless strangers walking in off the street asking to just pop up and see Mr Graves about this or that. I swear some of them were criminals! I once had a vagrant come in and ask to go up. I informed him he must make an appointment and he tried to tell me that was not the way Miss Jones had handled things. Well, I told him quite rightly that Miss Jones had a lot to answer for and it was about time someone such as myself put things straight. He didn't like that."

"No, I suppose he didn't."

"He made an appointment though," Dot looked pleased with herself. "People learn eventually. Miss Jones no doubt thought she was being a good Samaritan letting all and sundry wander in. But she did not consider Mr Graves. He would turn no one away and ran himself into the ground trying to help others. I made it my duty to monitor his appointments and reduce his workload. That was why I was so shocked when he died. I truly thought I had made a difference to his life with my little bits of assistance."

Dot almost looked affronted that Mr Graves had had the nerve to die on her watch.

"Did Mr Erikson get visitors walking in off the street?"

"No. Mr Erikson is much more proper. Mr Graves was always doing charity work. That was the trouble," Dot looked aggrieved. "I dare say he did a lot of good work, but there was no call to have all these random people wandering in. Some of them looked decidedly unsavoury."

"Were any of them regular visitors to his office?"

"No. In fact, after I made my feelings clear on the subject, Mr Graves took to hiring the village hall on a Wednesday morning, and would meet his charity cases there. They could just drop in and see him. I believe he was quite busy."

Clara marvelled that Isaac Graves had made a special arrangement to suit his fierce, and rather lacking in compassion, secretary. Though, she supposed, it would have made his charity clients feel better than having to brave the indomitable Miss Parker.

"On the morning of Mr Graves' sad demise, how did he seem?" Clara asked.

"His usual self," Dot shrugged. "Everyone asks that, as if I should have known he was about to die. He seemed perfectly normal to me."

"And his clients that morning, were any of them angry or upset after seeing Mr Graves."

"No," Dot held herself rigid in her seat as Bramble sniffed her shoe. "Mr Graves was very tactful. I never saw a client leave his office upset."

"So, you can't say if Mr Graves had any enemies? Clients who felt he had let them down, perhaps?"

"Mr Graves was always proper. No, none of his clients seemed disagreeable to me."

Except for the charity cases, Clara thought to herself.

"Did his family ever call at the offices?"

"On occasion. Usually his mother. She found it best to catch him in his office if she wanted to discuss something with him. I have met three of his sisters, too, but not the youngest, Julia. She has never paid a call to the offices in my time there. Quite frankly I am most relieved about that. I hear tell she has had quite the sordid past."

"When was the last time any of the family visited him?"

Dot took a moment to consider the question.

"I believe Mrs Graves came the week before his unfortunate..." Dot gave a little cough and didn't finish the sentence. "Yes, it would have been the Thursday or Friday before. She wanted to talk to Mr Graves."

"I don't suppose you know what about?"

"How would I?" Dot looked mortified. "I don't listen at doors Miss Fitzgerald!"

"No, I am sure. I just thought she might have mentioned something in passing?"

"I really couldn't say. Though she had said something about organising another charabanc tour for herself and the girls. That seems to be all she ever thinks about. She will have to curtail those now Mr Graves is no longer available to foot the bills," Dot's sneering attitude to everyone around her was beginning to get on Clara's nerves. Had someone slipped in to murder the unpleasant secretary she would quite have understood it. Mr Graves really seemed too nice for anybody to want to murder him. Perhaps that was why she was getting nowhere. She needed to understand Mr Graves better and maybe then she would know why someone wanted him dead.

"Tell me about Mr Graves," Clara said. "You must have known him quite well, give me an honest picture of him."

Dot hesitated. Honest pictures were not always the kindest, but if anyone had the nerve to tell Clara exactly what Mr Graves was like, it was his forthright secretary.

"He believed in helping others," Dot began generously. "He felt sorry for the poor. He rather made himself a martyr to the problems of the destitute."

"Tell me something I wouldn't read in the papers. Tell me about the real man," Clara pressed.

Dot shuffled in her seat. Her eyes flicked about the room. She was working up the nerve to say what she really thought.

"If he wasn't my employer…" she stopped herself.

"Go on, please. If he wasn't your employer…?"

Dot sighed, and then made up her mind.

"If he wasn't my employer I would have made a point of staying clear of him," Dot said firmly. "There was something about him that would give me the shivers. Something not quite right. I never heard he had done any wrong, and his clients were delighted with him. But as a person, as a man, there was something not quite right."

"How do you mean?"

"He… he made me feel uncomfortable when he was near me, but for no real reason. I used to have this awful fear that we would touch accidentally. The thought alone would make my skin crawl. But, you see, I can give you no reason for such feelings because he had never done me any harm. And, as far as I know, he had never done any harm to anyone."

"Perhaps you sensed something about him?"

"Perhaps," Dot was trying to explain herself and knew she was failing. "There was something wrong with him. In comparison to Mr Erikson, who I have never had any fears about, I always felt there was something sinister lurking behind Mr Graves' smile. As if he knew he was capable of doing harm to people, so he made a determined attempt to do as much good as possible to counter it. Have you ever owned a cat that for no apparent reason would suddenly sink its claws into you after rubbing itself against you? That was how Mr Graves felt."

This was a very interesting insight for Clara. But if Mr Graves was masking his real self all these years, how did that link to his murder? Unless someone was catching up with him for a crime committed years before. Clara suddenly thought of the death of Zachary Graves. Could it be that simple? Had Isaac murdered his father and, years later, someone had discovered the truth and killed him in the same fashion to make a point?

"I should really be going. My lunch break is only an hour," Dot was getting to her feet.

"Thank you for coming Miss Parker, and for being honest."

"That is perfectly all right, just so long as people don't think I was neglecting my duty."

"Of course not!"

After Dot had gone Clara sat in her chair staring at the file on Zachary Graves' death. She wondered if the coroner, or possibly the police detective, who had investigated the case was still alive? Now they might be useful people to talk to.

Chapter Eighteen

Clara decided it was time to regroup and assess where they stood on the Graves' case. Tommy and Annie had returned from their jaunts and had filled her in on their latest findings. Certain ideas were forming in Clara's mind, but without proof they would have to remain educated speculations.

"My hunch is that we are still looking to the family for our murderer," Clara started the debate. "There were certainly plenty of tensions there to explain a desire to harm the father."

"But the brother?" Tommy asked. "Aside from Miss Parker's observations, we have no real indication of a motive."

"Family secrets are often difficult to unearth," Clara mused. "This one appears to have been hidden for several decades. Perhaps Mr Graves realised, after all these years, that his father had been murdered and, just perhaps, he guessed who the murderer was."

"Maybe he was unwise enough to try to talk to the murderer?" Annie added. "People do foolish things when they are dealing with family."

"But would he be foolish enough to die in the same fashion as his father?" Clara said. "The key is the glass of water found on the desks of both men when they died. I think they drank something poisonous. But if Isaac had learned that his father had been murdered in such a way, would he blindly accept a glass of water from his father's killer?"

"Supposing he didn't know, that brings us back to the forged will being a motive," Tommy argued. "And that puts the spotlight firmly back on Julia Graves, she was the only one to benefit from the will."

"Surely that is too obvious?" Annie glanced between them both. "I swear to you that Julia was the only one of the Graves family who seemed genuinely distressed at her brother's death. I don't think she was acting."

"But who else would forge such a will?" Clara said. "Admittedly it was a somewhat clumsy forgery. The technical side was good, but the contents were always likely to raise suspicion. Something with more subtlety would have been safer to avoid detection."

"If it wasn't Julia, which I severely doubt," Tommy spoke, "then I would suggest we are looking for someone with a guilty conscience."

"A guilty conscience over Julia?"

"Yes."

"I suppose we have ruled out Mr Erikson in all this?" Annie suddenly interrupted. "I know it is an awful thing to say, seeing as he was the one who began this whole case, but he did have the opportunity."

"You really are beginning to think like a detective," Clara grinned at her. "As far as I can tell Mr Erikson has no motive, and embroiling us in this case, if he was the murderer, would be pretty foolish. Considering that no one had raised the suggestion of murder before he did. If he had killed Mr Graves, he would have been better off keeping quiet and not drawing attention to the crime."

They all agreed that was logical. Clara was just about to raise the subject of the stolen divorce papers when there was a knock on the front door. It sounded rather urgent and no one spoke as Annie hastened to answer it.

When she returned she looked pale.

"There is a policeman on the doorstep. He says Annabel Graves has just been rushed to hospital. She looks to be dying."

Clara jumped from her chair without thinking and almost fell to the floor.

"Damn foot!" she angrily cried at herself. "You must go at once, Annie!"

For an instant Annie hovered between rushing to Clara's aid and heading for her hat and coat. Clara shooed her off with a firm wave of her hand, she was almost back in her chair anyway. Annie ran to get her coat and then accompanied the policeman out the door.

Annie was shown to the third floor of the Brighton General Hospital and to one of the female wards. There was a lot of bustle occurring in the ward, and the presence of Inspector Park-Coombs told Annie everything she needed to know. She approached him rather nervously. The Inspector was rather intimidating, though Clara did not seem to think so. Annie, on the other hand, had a healthy respect for the police ingrained from childhood and found herself rather tongue-tied before Park-Coombs. He gave her a polite nod.

"Clara sent you?" he asked, needlessly. "This is a very puzzling matter."

Park-Coombs moved back so Annie could see the bed just beyond him. In it lay Annabel Graves. She was not breathing. A nurse was trying to find a pulse, while a doctor was standing to one side scratching his chin.

"She became ill with breathing difficulties," the Inspector elaborated. "I was summoned because she managed to hiss the word 'murder' to the ambulance men who brought her here. I thought I ought to inform Clara at once."

"She is dead?" Annie asked uneasily.

"Passed away shortly after arriving," Park-Coombs jumped into action as the doctor finished writing on a clipboard and began to move away from his patient.

"Doctor, if I could have a word?"

The doctor looked annoyed. He glanced at Annabel one last time, then gave a small sigh.

"If you must, Inspector."

Annie had only a moment to consider what Clara would do in the circumstances. She quickly tailed the Inspector as the doctor showed him to a side-room that served as an office. The doctor gave her a hard look as she slipped through the door behind him. Annie almost quailed and ran away, she also had a healthy respect for doctors. Thankfully, the Inspector came to her aid.

"My associate," he introduced Annie to the doctor. "You will take notes, won't you Miss Green?"

Annie realised he was giving her a valid excuse to be there. She quickly fumbled in her handbag for a small notebook and a pencil. Ripping out her shopping list, she started a fresh page and tried to look as if she often conducted secretarial duties, pencil poised in her hand.

The doctor seemed unconvinced, but he was not in the mood to argue. He had his rounds to attend to, along with a stack of paperwork. He wanted the inspector out of his office as swiftly as possible.

"Before you ask, without a post-mortem I am in no position to tell you how Miss Graves died," he said, choosing not to take the seat behind his desk, but to stand.

"You must have made a tentative diagnosis of her condition before she died?" Park-Coombs asked, slipping into the calm, questioning manner reserved for people who irritated him. He would keep the doctor busy all afternoon if he chose, and his voice implied this.

"Look, she was suffering from breathing difficulties."

"Caused by what?"

The doctor harrumphed.

"We had yet to determine that when the patient passed."

"You must have had a suspicion, though? Or do you wait to diagnose all your patients by post-mortem?"

Now the doctor was offended.

"Look here, don't imply I can't do my job!"

"Then perhaps you will be kind enough to understand that I am only doing mine? A woman cries murder as she dies, that makes it my duty to investigate."

The doctor made a dismissive noise, but he did at last take a chair.

"I have barely had a chance to look at the patient's file," he said, his voice a little less aggressive. "I was called because a woman was having problems breathing. Her throat was swollen almost shut. Her tongue was enlarged. Her heart was racing and her pulse was erratic. According to the ambulance men the condition had come on extremely rapidly. Within minutes of her arrival the patient's heart stopped, I would suggest caused by asphyxia due to the swelling of the throat. Though that is a mere hypothesis until the post-mortem is done."

"She suffocated?" the Inspector looked perplexed. "How?"

"I would imagine she had a deadly reaction to something. As I say I have not seen the patient's files, so I don't know if she had a history of asthma. A severe asthma attack can kill a person."

"Excuse me, Doctor?" Annie made the title sound very formal. "But could it have been poison?"

The doctor gave Annie a strange look.

"There have been two highly suspicious deaths within the ranks of the Graves family already," Park-Coombs came to her assistance. "A third seems an unlikely coincidence."

The doctor seemed to give a little jolt of surprise.

"Two? Why, I had heard Isaac Graves' death was sudden, but not that it was suspicious."

"You must be the only soul in Brighton not to have heard then," the Inspector joked morbidly. "Please answer Miss Green's question."

"We do see quite a few cases of poisoning. Usually accidental," the doctor assured them hastily. "But, I have to say, the common poisons show symptoms other than just asphyxia. For instance, Strychnine poisoning can cause suffocation, but it is accompanied by seizures and muscles spasms. Neither of which Miss Graves demonstrated."

There was a tap on the door and an orderly appeared with a file in his hand. He gave it to the doctor then left.

"This is Miss Graves' file," the doctor said, opening the folder to scan the contents. He gave a small sigh. "No history of asthma."

"That is one theory out the window," Inspector Park-Coombs sounded rather satisfied. "So, come on doctor, what do you think killed the woman? If not poison or asthma, why does someone suddenly stop breathing?"

The doctor rapped his fingers on the top of the desk. He was clearly feeling rather defensive before the dogged inspector. He wanted to give an answer, so that he didn't look a fool.

"My surmise is she had an acute reaction to something."

"We have already ruled out poisoning," Park-Coombs reminded him.

"Some people can have deadly reactions to substances that are not normally considered poisonous," the doctor said a little aggressively. "I have a man in Ward 2, for instance, who nearly died after being stung by a bee. He had the exact same symptoms, most notably an inability to breathe."

Now Park-Coombs was interested.

"I have never heard of a man dying from a bee sting before."

"He suffers from an acute allergy. Admittedly when a bee stings it is injecting a form of poison into its victim. But, for the most part, people are not harmed by this poison. We merely feel the pain. But some unfortunate souls develop a deadly reaction to the sting. We don't know why."

"But this man survived?"

"Just. We have no means for reversing the reaction. All we can do is stabilise the patient and treat the symptoms. We came close to losing him."

"What sort of things can people be allergic to?" Annie asked.

"No one really knows the answer to that. I suppose just about anything a person can ingest or that can somehow enter the body."

"My wife can't eat peaches," Park-Coombs mused. "They give her dreadful wind. Yet, most people eat peaches without complaint."

"An allergy is usually more severe than that," the doctor begrudged Park-Coombs his insight. "In general the reactions will be deadly."

"And, can it run in families?" Annie persisted.

The doctor looked tired with the conversation. He scratched at his head.

"As I said, I have not studied the subject in depth. But, yes, it could be possible. Many such things run in families."

"What an innocuous way to kill someone," the Inspector said, startling Annie and the doctor. "How would you ever prove such a thing was murder rather than an accident?"

"That is not my department," the doctor said firmly. "Now, if you don't mind, I have living patients to attend to."

"Naturally, doctor," Park-Coombs gave him a rather sinister grin. "You return to the living and I'll stick around with the dead. They, after all, are my department."

The doctor looked a little disturbed. He picked the file up from the desk and let himself out of the office.

"I would suggest, Miss Green, that you make a very hasty trip to the Graves' home," Park-Coombs said as soon as he was gone.

Annie looked up at the detective rather startled.

"Why?"

"Because I am about to place a phone call summoning

155

the entire family to the hospital, and while they are here, dealing with the endless paperwork and questions I will sadly have to subject them to, you will be searching their home for evidence."

"Evidence? What sort of evidence?" Annie looked worried.

"Miss Graves had an allergic reaction to something. I imagine the substance was placed in her food or, possibly, a glass of water. Do you take my meaning?"

Annie did.

"You want me to look for something odd or out-of-place that might have been used to poison her?"

"Not poison, Annie. This is a substance that under normal circumstances would be perfectly harmless. Since I don't think we are looking at a bee sting, I would suggest something edible."

Annie began thinking of her own kitchen. What substances did she have on her shelves or in cupboards that could easily and innocuously be added to a glass of water without being noticed?

"It would have to be colourless to go in water, and virtually tasteless," she said aloud.

"I would say, more importantly, it must be scentless. Taste is less relevant, as once the person has ingested it, it is already too late."

"It could be just about anything," Annie said, suddenly feeling anxious.

"True, I am sending you to find a needle in a haystack. But, let's hope for a little serendipity. Or rather, let's hope our killer has grown rather cocky and careless. After all, they have already gotten away with two murders."

Annie was worried, but, at the same time, she was determined to do as the Inspector asked.

"It will take me at least half an hour to get to the house."

"Do not fear, Miss Green, I shall have the Graves ladies tied up here all afternoon."

Annie picked up her bag and started out the door. She

hesitated for a moment.

"Tell your wife to try cooking the peaches next time she fancies eating them, and adding a little sugar to the pan," this piece of culinary knowledge satisfactorily dispensed, Annie headed out of the hospital to track down a mysterious, killer substance.

Chapter Nineteen

The Inspector had been good to his word. There was no one at home except for the Graves' maid when Annie arrived at the house. She paused on the doorstep. What, precisely, was she supposed to say to the maid? Clara would invent some suitable white lie. Annie was not so good at invention. After dawdling for a moment, she decided she would appeal to the maid's sense of duty and be honest. As a fellow servant, hopefully the maid would be amenable to helping.

Annie rang the bell. After a mere instant (suggesting the maid had been nearby) the door opened and a girl of about nineteen appeared.

"Terribly sorry, miss, all the ladies are out."

"I know," Annie told her. "I am afraid I have come on a rather difficult errand. Might I confide in you…"

Annie left a pause for the girl to insert her name. Obediently the maid responded.

"Glynis."

"Glynis, dear, something awful has happened."

"I know. Miss Annabel was taken queer," Glynis' eyes widened in memory of the horror. "It was awful. I was just going past her bedroom when I heard her choking and trying to call for help."

"I'm sure your intervention was timely, but sadly Annabel Graves passed away in the hospital a mere hour ago."

Glynis gave a gasp.

"Was she dreadfully ill then?"

"Glynis, you must keep this extremely secret, but, before she passed, Annabel claimed she had been murdered."

The little maid almost stumbled backwards in shock. It took a moment for this news to sink in.

"But… how?"

"That is what I have been sent here to find out. May I come in?"

"I… I don't understand," Glynis was flustered, but she held her ground by the door.

"Glynis, your mistress was poisoned, but by a substance that is normally harmless. She had an unusual reaction to something that other people would take and find perfectly safe. Now, I have been sent to search for this substance by the police."

"I keep the arsenic locked up," Glynis was trembling a little, perhaps expecting the blame to fall upon her. It had to be said that when a member of a well-to-do household was poisoned (whether deliberately or accidentally) the servants usually took the blame. Glynis was clearly thinking she was being accused of something.

"It was not arsenic. In fact, it was not something that would look like a poison to me or you."

"Then, how…?"

"Glynis, is there any sort of food that disagrees with you?"

Glynis was puzzled by the change of subject, but she answered all the same.

"I can't drink cow's milk, miss, never could. As a babe I was given goat's milk."

"I imagine cow's milk makes you unwell?"

"Gives me gripe something rotten, and I can't keep off the toilet," Glynis admitted.

"Well, just like you are intolerant to milk, so Annabel Graves was intolerant to something. Something ordinary. Except, in her case, the substance made her dangerously ill."

Glynis was finally getting to grips with the idea Annie was explaining.

"So, she weren't deliberately poisoned?"

"That all depends on whether someone knew she would have a fatal reaction to the substance. That is why we must search the house, Glynis, and see if there is anything odd or amiss. We should start with the bedroom."

"And the police said to do this?" Glynis asked cautiously, she was not as naïve as might be imagined.

"Inspector Park-Coombs himself instructed me to come," Annie confirmed.

After a short moment of indecision, Glynis stepped back from the door and showed Annie inside.

"This way to the bedroom, miss," she escorted Annie up a short set of stairs and onto a landing, before turning off to the right. She pushed open a door and they walked into Annabel Graves' bedroom.

"She was slumped at her dressing table," Glynis said, giving a little shiver as she remembered the scene. "I knew she were ill. But I didn't expect her to die."

Annie went to the dressing table and looked at its surface. A silver-backed hairbrush appeared to have been thrown down in haste, there were ribbons and hairpins scattered around it and a pair of spectacles tossed to one side.

"Is this how the dressing table looked when you came in?" Annie asked Glynis.

The girl's face clouded.

"I suppose so, I didn't really look."

"Have you been in here since?"

"Only to tidy up a little before Miss Annabel came home..." Glynis stopped herself and there was a moment when Annie wondered if she would descend into tears.

Then she rallied. "If someone killed her, that was a dastardly thing to do, miss."

"Yes, it was. Have you moved anything on this dressing table?"

Glynis glanced at the assortment of hairpins and ribbons. She had been tidying in a daze, still shocked by the sudden illness of Miss Annabel.

"I brushed up some face powder that had been spilt and removed Miss Annabel's water glass."

Annie's ears pricked up.

"A water glass?"

"Yes. It is kept on the nightstand normally, but I suppose she had brought it over here with her," Glynis pointed to a nightstand near the bed where a now empty and clean glass stood next to a water jug. There was no chance of discovering if something had been placed in the glass of water now, unless the killer had poisoned the entire water jug.

"Is that the water Annabel had overnight?"

"Oh no, miss. I tipped that out and put in fresh for when she returned."

Foiled again, Annie sighed. But here was a clue at least. A third member of the Graves' family had died with a glass of water at their hand. Whatever the dangerous substance was, it was definitely something that could be slipped into a glass of water without being noticed.

"I must look in the other bedrooms," Annie said, she was confident the killer would not be stupid enough to leave the poison in Annabel's room. Especially with suspicion hanging over the death of Isaac Graves. But they had to have hidden it somewhere. "We must look for a vial or bottle."

Glynis looked worried, but showed Annie into Mrs Graves' bedroom nonetheless. The room smelt stuffily of lavender and decaying roses. The curtains were barely drawn. Annie promptly pulled them fully back. Then they began to search; looking in boxes, opening drawers, even hunting beneath the bed. Glynis picked up a bottle containing oil of roses, which explained the smell in the room. Annie shook her head. It would smell too strongly. There was nothing more to be found in Mrs Graves' room so they moved on to the room of Christiana Graves. Christiana liked books, especially on astronomy, and the room was lined with shelves. They hunted everywhere they could think of, but aside from a pill box containing aspirin there was nothing to discover.

They moved on to Julia's room. The youngest Graves daughter had an impressive medicine chest sitting on her dressing table.

"Miss Julia does suffer with her ailments," Glynis explained as Annie opened the cabinet and saw a standard array of treatments.

"What sort of ailments?" she asked.

"Oh, I could write you a list! Headaches, rheumatics, indigestion and certain feminine complaints."

Annie glanced up, prompting Glynis to add.

"The sort my mother used to get, and she would complain how it was the perils of having children. I always thought it rather odd Miss Julia having the same, considering she was never married."

Annie did not enlighten Glynis; certain secrets were best kept quiet. Annie looked through the medicines, but nothing struck her as poisonous in the manner she was looking for. She picked up a bottle labelled 'essence of cloves'.

"Miss Julia is a bit of a herbalist. She has studied the subject. She knows how to make up a lot of herbal remedies. She showed me how to make a mint tea for aiding the digestion," Glynis helpfully explained.

Annie opened the bottle, but it had been empty some time. The remaining contents had long ago dried up. As tempting as the medicine cabinet was, it clearly did not offer the solution. Annie shut it up and turned the key in the lock, then she followed Glynis into Agatha's bedroom. They performed a thorough search of the contents; every drawer was opened, every hiding place examined, but there was no sign of anything suspicious. Annie felt she had reached a dead-end. The killer had to have hidden the poison somewhere, but, as the Inspector had said, it was like looking for a needle in a haystack.

Annie and Glynis returned to the hallway and the little maid ensured the bedroom doors were shut behind them. Annie was about to head downstairs and conduct a search of the lower rooms when her eye glimpsed a door to their right.

"What room is that?" she asked Glynis.

"Oh, that is poor Mr Graves' old room. Mr Isaac Graves, I mean. The family kept it as it was when he lived here, in case he ever wanted to stay over. Which he rarely did," Glynis shrugged at the foibles of people who had so many rooms in their house, that they were able to leave one unoccupied. She clearly came from a home where space was at a premium and privacy a thing unheard of.

Annie went to the room and turned the door handle.

"Oh, it will be locked miss…" Glynis tailed off as the door opened.

Annie looked at her.

"Locked?"

"Always. I have the key downstairs on a hook," Glynis had that worried look on her face again.

"I would say someone has been in here very recently, and in haste too. So hasty, in fact, they have neglected to lock the door again," Annie entered Isaac Graves' old bedroom.

It had the air of a guest bedroom. One that was rarely used and presented an appearance of formal tidiness. There were none of the signs of a room that is lived in; no book left carelessly on the nightstand, no dropped sock or discarded tie on the floor, none of the paraphernalia that is found in a person's regularly used bedroom. Yet, Annie sensed with an instinct that only a servant could possess and understand, that someone had been in the room recently. She looked around her, certain there was something there that she should see. It was Glynis who

163

in fact spotted the clue.

"The sticky drawer is open," Glynis automatically went to the top drawer of an old-fashioned dresser and gave it a firm push.

Annie followed her and stared at the drawer.

"I presume you would never leave the drawer like that?"

"No, miss," Glynis paused. "Though, to be honest, I never open that drawer as a rule. I come in once a week to dust, but that is all. Mr Graves kept some old photographs in there. I believe last time I had cause to open it was when Mrs Graves was looking for a picture to place in the paper, when poor Mr Graves died. That was when I discovered it didn't close properly unless you gave it a good push."

"Glynis, open the drawer again."

Glynis did so, and they both looked inside. As Glynis had stated, there was a pile of photographs in the small drawer, all of Mr Graves at various stages in his life. But right on top, sitting on a picture of Isaac Graves as a lad at school, was a small glass vial. Annie picked it up very carefully in her handkerchief. It was not labelled, but it did contain liquid. It was an oily brown colour.

"What is it?" Glynis asked.

"I don't know," Annie admitted. "But, the way it was hidden, I think this could be our killer substance."

She moved the vial in the light and the oil slid slowly along the glass.

"I must take this back to the Inspector," Annie pocketed the bottle. "Glynis, say nothing about my visit to your employers and keep your eyes and ears open for anything suspicious."

"I will do. I can't bear the thought of Miss Annabel being killed. She was a nice woman. She liked to help with the cooking."

"Did she now?"

"Yes. She often would be in my larder seeing what ingredients we had to hand. She liked fruit cake."

Annie wondered if Annabel's forays into the larder were also an excuse to ensure nothing hazardous to her health had been accidentally bought. That is, if Annabel even knew she had a deadly allergy.

"Glynis, were you ever told not to buy anything for the larder? Perhaps there was something the family expressed a dislike to?"

Glynis considered this.

"I don't recall anything in particular," she said with a shrug. "I was usually given a shopping list anyway, except for the essentials, you know, flour and such."

"Thank you again, Glynis. Hopefully your cooperation will help find Miss Annabel's killer."

"I do hope so, miss," Glynis was downcast. "To think she just died like that."

Annie left Glynis mulling over the vagaries of life, determined to hasten as fast as she could back to Brighton. She walked to the nearest omnibus stop, but the timetable indicated she had missed the last one. Grumbling to herself she set to walking again. Her thoughts were on food. More specifically on how food could kill you. It was a frightening thought. As far as Annie knew there was no food that particularly disagreed with her, though, after this incident, she would be much more cautious about trying some of the fancy foods coming across from the Continent. Clara and Tommy were rather taken by this foreign stuff, but who was to say if it suddenly might prove that one of them was deadly allergic to it? Annie gave a shudder. Only the other month Tommy had insisted on trying this peculiar foreign cheese, which was all yellow and runny and you had to cook in the oven! Annie had never heard of such a strange cheese, though it was from France and the French did have odd ideas. Annie decided that, from now on, she was clamping down on this foreign food malarkey. After all, she didn't know anyone who had died from eating English beef or, for that matter, a good bit of brawn. No, there was no question about it. Whatever was in the vial in her pocket must be from foreign climes. How it had come into the Graves' possession was a question for Clara to answer.

It took Annie an hour to make her way to the police station and her feet hurt considerably when she arrived. She asked the Desk Sergeant for Inspector Park-Coombs. The Sergeant was usually quite belligerent to Clara, but he did not know who Annie was, and when she explained she had been sent on an errand for the Inspector he assumed she was a servant. The Inspector was summoned.

"What did you find?" he asked as he came down the stairs.

"I think this is it," Annie handed him the vial. "It doesn't have a label and was hidden in a drawer."

The Inspector took the bottle.

"Thank you, Annie. I shall have our boys look at it at once. You look a little flushed, are you all right?"

"I am perfectly fine, Inspector. Though I expect my mutton pie is burnt to a cinder by now. Those two will not have checked on it," Annie gave a heavy-hearted sigh. "Food, Inspector. This all comes back to food."

With that remark Annie left the station to see if she could salvage supper.

Chapter Twenty

Clara was beginning to wonder what had become of Annie, when there was a knock on the door and she went to investigate. There was a woman on the doorstep. She was in her early twenties, but heavily made up and smoking a cheap cigarette. Clara leaned on her walking stick awkwardly as she looked at the stranger.

"Hello?"

"Clara Fitzgerald?" the woman asked, the cigarette not leaving her mouth.

"Yes?"

"Rose Hart. I need to talk with you."

Clara had an awful thought that she might be about to become engaged in another case. It was bad enough being unable to investigate one, let alone to have two cases niggling away at her. But Clara was not one to turn a person away who needed help.

"Come in," she said, shuffling back from the door.

Rose Hart entered and surveyed the hallway as if she was considering buying the house.

"What did you do to your foot?"

Clara was a little surprised by the question. The news of her accident had been quite the talk of Brighton, considering the circumstances, and anyone who knew her name almost certainly had heard of her misfortune.

"I was run over by a hearse," Clara answered as she shut the door.

Rose Hart chuckled.

"That must have been pretty unlucky!"

"It was," Clara admitted. "Do go through into the parlour."

Rose escorted herself into the parlour, leaving Clara to trail behind. She continued to survey the house and its possessions as if she was weighing it up for some reason. It made Clara feel uncomfortable, as if Rose knew something she didn't.

"I have that print too," Rose suddenly pointed to a small framed postcard-sized print of the Brighton Pavilion. They had been sold as part of fundraising efforts by the committee last year. Clara, as a new member of the committee, had seen it as her duty to buy one. They had only been going for a few pence, one of the cheaper items on sale. The whole idea was that everyone in the community could help support the Pavilion, not just the wealthy. The print had been extremely popular and they had sold over 1,000 copies.

"Mine ain't framed though," Rose continued on merrily enough. "I just pinned it to the wall of my room."

"Would you like a seat? I would offer to make tea...?"

"No, love, I can see you ain't able," Rose flopped herself down into a chair. "I'm surprised in a big house like this you ain't got a maid."

"She is out," Clara said honestly, though she suspected Rose disbelieved her.

She lowered herself awkwardly into a chair and groaned a little as the weight came off her foot.

"Broken, is it?" Rose asked.

"Yes. Though apparently it could have been worse. Doctors always like to tell you when things could have been worse."

"Supposed to make you feel better," Rose nodded. "I keep away from doctors."

"I didn't have much option," Clara smiled. "It serves me right for trying to rescue someone's hat for them."

Rose laughed again. It was a nice laugh, a tad loud, but genuine.

"The Inspector said you was housebound and I ought to pay you a call."

"The Inspector?"

"Park-Coombs. Funny fellow, bit too nice to be a policeman, I always reckon."

"I prefer my policemen that way."

"Yeah, I suppose…" Rose paused and stared at the Pavilion print again. "Anyway, he came to pay me a call. I told him I ain't done nothing wrong in weeks. I has a proper job now in a sweet factory. He ain't got no call harassing me, and then he explained that you would like to talk to me."

Clara was confused.

"Rose, I do apologise, but could you explain that to me again? Why did the Inspector call on you?"

Rose rolled her eyes, clearly thinking that Clara was a penny short of tuppence.

"The Inspector says you are investigating the death of Mr Isaac Graves, since it might be murder like. Oh, I just realised whose hearse ran you over!" Rose giggled again. "You poor soul. Anyway, the Inspector says you are trying to find out about Mr Graves and I could help because I made a complaint against him. That was brave of me, because normally girls like myself stay clear of the police."

Clara suddenly realised who Rose Hart was.

"You are the girl who complained that Mr Graves was being too friendly while you were in the Ladies' House of Reform?"

"That's right. I wasn't taken none too seriously at first. The police don't like it when an 'upstanding member of the community' is accused of being saucy with a working girl, even if she is trying to improve her lot. That Inspector, though, he listened to me. He said he would

169

have words and make sure Mr Graves never came near me again. And that is what he did. That's why I didn't slam the door in his face when he turned up on my doorstep."

Clara now fully understood who she was talking to and why she was there.

"Did the Inspector explain that I believe Mr Graves was murdered?"

"He did. I told him, I didn't do it!" Rose laughed.

"No, I never thought you did. But I am interested to know more about Mr Graves. His secretary said there was something... uncomfortable about him?"

"Yeah, she was right. Like, you didn't want him touching you," Rose became conspiratorial. "Now, I have not led an upstanding life, and I have known quite a few men in my time. Some were all right, some were not. But only a handful made me feel truly uneasy. Mr Graves was one of them."

"Do you mean he seemed dangerous?" Clara asked, trying to understand exactly what it was about Isaac Graves that had caused this woman such discomfort.

"Not in the sense that I thought he was going to hit me, or anything," Rose answered. "I mean, I had this fellow once who pulled a knife on me. He scared the living daylights out of me! They never caught him, you know. I swear he was a killer if ever I saw one, but who gives a toss what a girl like me says?"

"Then, what was it about Mr Graves?"

"He was..." Rose paused to find the right word. "Slimy. Yeah, that's it. If he touched you, you felt dirty. I imagined he was the sort of fellow who would be into strange stuff. A girl like me sees that sort. Men who want a little more than just the basics."

"Mr Graves was never a client though?"

"No. Look, I ain't going to lie about my past. The Inspector said you would understand. You know why I was in the House of Reform. I spent five years on the streets before that. So, when I say I know a thing or two about men and their cravings, I think we can agree I know what I am talking about."

"I don't doubt that for an instant," Clara assured her. "Nor will I judge you for your past. I am just curious, because I only barely knew Mr Graves before his untimely demise. And it is very difficult to assess a man's personality after he stops breathing."

Rose gave a chuckle.

"You are a good sort!" she laughed. "I can see why you are a detective. Must be hard making your way in a man's world. Do you get a lot of resentment?"

"From time to time, and not just from men. But that isn't going to stop me."

"Good for you! So what else can I tell you about Mr Graves?"

Clara felt she had Rose's trust now, or as much trust as Rose ever gave anyone. It was time to probe deeper.

"Can you tell me exactly what occurred between you and Mr Graves that made you go to the police? I imagine that was not a decision taken lightly?"

"No, it wasn't," Rose gave a sigh. "Look, I had been on the streets since I was barely out of school. It was never a fun nor easy life. Some of the older ladies would take pity on you and give you a hand, but quite often their solution to problems was a bottle of gin. I saw quite quickly that I was doomed to end up like them if I didn't try to change. But how is a girl like me to change? You can't just walk into a shop and ask for a job. Anyhow, I had more immediate concerns, like how to keep a roof over my head. The only thing I swore to myself was never to take to the bottle. I hoped I could maybe earn enough to improve my lot. The other girls spent all their money on drink, then they had nothing and never would have. My mother was a drinker. I weren't going to end up like that."

"How did you learn about the House of Reform?" Clara asked.

"During the war we had these women police on the

streets. Only they weren't police, exactly, as they were volunteers and couldn't arrest you. But they wanted to get the girls off the streets. Most of 'em didn't give a damn about us girls. Their concern was that we might give some disease to the soldiers from the nearby camps. Do you remember the military camp near Brighton?"

"I do," Clara nodded. "I remember all the lads coming into town in their uniforms."

"Those were grand days!" Rose said wistfully. "Not the war, mind! But all the lads. I think that was the only time I came close to being happy in my work. So many fresh, young faces. It used to break my heart though to think of them going off to fight. So many didn't come back."

Rose shook off the dark memories.

"So these women police, I think they called themselves patrols? Anyway, they would try and chase you off the streets mostly, but one or two actually wanted to help. One of these gave me a leaflet and pointed me in the direction of the House of Reform. I wasn't sure about it, but she persuaded me that it would change my life, and I really did want to get off the streets. So I went to them and I told 'em my story, and they took me in. That was 1917."

"When did you first meet Mr Graves?"

"I think it would be the Christmas of that year. We had a party. We all chipped in to make things. Mr Graves attended along with the other members on the House of Reform Board. I remember he kept looking at me, as if he recognised me. I certainly had never seen him before. Later I said to the other girls about him, but none reckoned he had ever visited them. So I wasn't sure what to make of it," Rose gave a little shiver. "Couple of months later he caught me alone in the House. I was studying for a religious lesson I was supposed to be helping with. We were all encouraged to participate in educating each other. I was in the back parlour, sitting by the fire and going through a pamphlet the teacher had given me, when he walked in. He said he wanted to talk to me, in private. Now, we are never supposed to be alone with men in the House. Not even the male teachers. I was a little startled, but I didn't like to leave, as he was such an important person on the Board."

"What happened?"

"He started asking me all these questions, not even with any explanation! He wanted to know how old I was. When was my birthday? Who were my parents? How I ended up on the streets? Well, how was I to explain all that? I was adopted, you see. I can only say that my mother claimed my birthday was 5 June 1898. That may have been true or not. Father died from tuberculosis when I was five, mother took to drink. I came home one day and found her dead at the kitchen table. I had nowhere to go and ended up on the streets.

"All this seemed to upset Mr Graves greatly. He began to pace about and ramble. He scared me a little, I don't mind saying. He kept saying he was sorry, but I had no idea for what and for an awful moment I thought he was going to do something to me and was apologising in advance. Then he sat next to me, so awfully close. And he said the weirdest thing! He said I was the spitting image of my mother! How did he know my mother? Then he started to reach out for my hand and I panicked. I jumped up, told him to leave me alone and fled for matron. Fortunately, she could see I was in a state and believed my story. She persuaded me to go to the police, for what little good it did. At least Mr Graves was banned from the House for a while."

"He said you were the spitting image of your mother?" Clara said, a dark thought swirling into her mind.

"But he didn't know my mother. Else, why was he asking me who my parents were?"

"Maybe he didn't mean your adopted mother," Clara mused. "Do you know anything about your real mother?"

"Not much," Rose admitted. "Only, when mother – my adopted mother – started to drink, she would say things. If I upset her she would say all sorts of nasty things. She once said I was the daughter of a whore. Another time she said she should never have gone to that house to pick up a baby. Only later, when I knew about the House of Reform, did I wonder if she was referring to that? But I don't know for sure. She might have meant any ordinary house. It was just an odd thing to say."

"Did your mother have adoption papers?" Clara asked.

"Yes. Don't know where they are now, but she used to pull them out of a box and wave them at me when she was angry. Just so I couldn't forget I was adopted."

"Then the adoption was through some organisation. That makes it unlikely she was referring to an ordinary house from which she had privately adopted you."

Rose gave a grin.

"Yes. That makes a lot of sense. But what does it all mean?"

"At this point I cannot say. But I do appreciate you taking the time to come out and talk to me."

"It was no bother," Rose shrugged. "I hope your foot feels better soon."

"Thank you, so do I."

After Rose had gone, Clara sat down and mulled over this new information. Could it be that she had just been talking to the daughter of Julia Graves? It would have been around 1898 that Julia went to the House of Reform, by 1899 her father was dead and could not have sent her. Could that also be a clue as to why he was killed? Resentment? Revenge? And it seemed Isaac Graves was in on the secret. He had seen Rose and spotted the resemblance to his sister when she was younger. It would be interesting to get an old photograph of Julia and see how she compared to her daughter. But if Isaac had found the child his sister had borne during her disgrace, it appeared he had not followed up the situation. And was this a clue to why he was killed, or merely a coincidence? Clara would have to research the matter further.

She was just about to make a phone call to the House of Reform to discover how she could access their records

when Annie walked in the door. She looked pale as she
stood in the parlour doorway and gave a sigh;
    "It looks like Annabel Graves has been murdered."

Chapter Twenty-one

At 4pm the next day, Inspector Park-Coombs and the coroner, Dr Deàth, obligingly paid a call on Clara. She arranged afternoon tea with scones and cucumber sandwiches. She was, after all, extremely grateful that the two men were considerate enough to take time away from their duties to visit her and update her on the case of Annabel Graves.

Dr Deàth was a familiar face to Clara. She had met him on her very first murder case, when she had gone to the morgue to identify a tramp who had died in the winter snows. Dr Deàth was the sort of man who enjoyed his job almost as much as he enjoyed life. He rarely seemed downhearted by the corpses in his morgue or the fragility of this mortal existence. In fact, he was rather jovial. He did, however, have the unfortunate habit of discussing his work rather a lot, which made him an awkward dinner party guest.

He walked in Clara's front door and spotted Bramble at once.

"Hello," he smiled at the dog, patting its head lightly. "Why, I have just done an autopsy on an old lady whose death is being blamed on a little dog, just like you, by her family."

"Really?" Clara asked.

"Why, yes. The old lady had a little black poodle, which had the unfortunate, but completely natural, habit of cat chasing. One morning this little dog darted after a cat, pulling its lead from the old woman's hand. The cat was across the road and the dog ran towards it, just as a milk cart was coming along. The old woman ran to follow, as fast as an old lady can manage, at least, and was struck down by the milk cart horse. She was taken to the hospital but sadly died and arrived in my department," Dr Deàth explained all this with an easy smile. Life's little accidents did not trouble him. "Cause of death was a blood clot in the brain. It was very speedy. The milkman was beside himself, but it was really not his fault. She stepped out right in front of him."

"And the dog?" Clara was looking suspiciously at Bramble.

"Not been seen since. Probably just as well. The family were not particularly fond of it from what I can tell. Would probably take it to the nearest veterinary surgeon to be destroyed."

"And this happened recently?"

"Two weeks ago. I believe there was a small piece in the papers. The funeral is in a couple of days' time. I had to get the body ready this morning for the undertakers. By the way, your little accident with the hearse is quite the talk among those of us who deal with the dead. Mr Clark will never forgive himself."

Clara was only half-listening. She was eyeing up a certain little black dog that was now looking rather sheepish.

"How is the foot?" Inspector Park-Coombs interjected.

"Sore," Clara answered. "Perhaps we could sit?"

She escorted them through to the parlour where Annie had laid out a fine spread on the table. Tommy was waiting for them, as was Annie, who Clara insisted should be present as this was as much her case as Clara's. The tea was brewing and the Inspector and Dr Deàth were offered scones. For a few moments everyone was busy with butter and homemade jam.

"What is the news concerning Annabel Graves?" Clara asked, once the ritual of tea pouring had been completed and everyone was munching into scones.

"She is definitely dead," Dr Deàth smiled.

There was an awkward pause. Fortunately, Dr Deàth was rather used to this.

"Coroner's humour," he explained. "It is the sort of thing that always raises a giggle in a busy mortuary, though not from the customers, of course."

Clara hastened to change the subject.

"You have had a chance to examine her?"

"Yes," Dr Deàth nodded. "Her death was very similar to her brother's. No real sign of disease or a cause. A slight inflammation of the throat and a blue tinge to the lips. Had you not suspected some unusual agent in the case, I would have recorded it as natural, probably a heart attack. Seems to run in the family."

Dr Deàth threw in the last comment with an ironic wink.

"And the vial Annie found?" Clara asked.

"Yes, the vial. That had the lab boys in a tizzy," the Inspector grinned, his opinion of the 'lab boys' (in fact a small trio of scientists housed at the Brighton station due to them having the space for a lab, and responsible for all manner of forensic tests for the entire county) was rather on the low side. Park-Coombs was not a man against science, but he rather felt it got in the way of general police work. Also, he always felt the lab boys were deliberately talking in gobbledygook to make him look stupid. "They tested it for all the usuals. Arsenic, strychnine, cocaine, morphine. Everything was negative. I told them we were not necessarily looking at a normally poisonous substance, rather one that most people would find harmless. That sent them in a new direction. It was clearly a refined oil, so they began looking at the range of natural oils available for purchase. After rather a fruitless string of tests, someone had the idea of tasting the substance. I suppose they were by now confident it was not poisonous, and equally I was breathing down their necks," Park-Coombs' smile broadened. "Someone tasted it, anyway, and discovered that it had a nutty flavour. That narrowed the search and they began exploring various types of nut oils."

"Nut oils?" Annie asked, looking concerned that there was a cooking ingredient she had not heard of.

"Yes, if you refine nuts you can extract oil," Dr Deàth confirmed. "It is very popular in Eastern cooking."

"Ah, so it's a foreign thing then?" Annie said, marginally relieved.

"I believe the Americans are experimenting with cooking oils too," Dr Deàth continued. "And the Italians have had olive oil for centuries."

Annie still looked worried.

"Were they able to identify precisely what type of oil it was?" Clara interrupted.

"They did," Park-Coombs said. "It took them several hours, but at long last I received a report that the mysterious substance was peanut oil."

"Peanuts?" Clara said in surprise.

"I haven't eaten peanuts in years," Tommy scraped jam onto his last chunk of scone. "You used to be able to buy a bag of them at the circus to eat or throw to the elephants. They come in those big egg-timer shaped shells, remember Clara?"

Clara was trying to visualise a peanut, but was struggling.

"They are also sometimes called Monkey Nuts. I believe the Americans are quite fond of having them salted," Dr Deàth explained. "I too recall having a bag at the circus many years ago. But they were a nuisance as you had to break open such large shells for such a very small nut. Personally, I'll stick with walnuts at Christmas."

"Can you still buy peanuts over here?" Clara could just

remember being handed a bag of large dimpled objects when she was a child at the fair, and being instructed on how to break the shells and extract the nuts. Most of hers went to an obliging monkey that seemed rather fond of them, and a whole lot better at breaking the shell than she was.

"I sent some officers out to discover that," Park-Coombs nodded. "During the war they were difficult to come by, just like everything else. But, in the last couple of years, America has been exporting a lot more goods in this direction. Even so, my men found no shops in Brighton selling them. I am extending the search wider. London is my next port of call."

"And you can extract an oil from these nuts?" Clara persisted.

"Yes. It is used in Asian cooking," Park-Coombs elaborated. "Or so my lab boys tell me. It is very rare."

"If it is used in cooking, it is not poisonous?" Annie was still feeling baffled about the idea of cooking with oil, rather than lard or butter.

"Not to most people," Dr Deàth told her. "But I conducted my own investigations after hearing Clara's suspicions. I rang some colleagues in London and asked them if they knew of any cases of people suffering fatal reactions from otherwise harmless food substances. I explained I was not looking for cases of food poisoning. After making a few calls I finally came across an old medical friend who knew of just such a case. Curiously, the person in question had suffered a fatal reaction to peanuts. I learned of this before I had even heard of the findings from the lab.

"According to my colleague, a British gentleman was dining out with friends and they decided to visit an Oriental restaurant. Before they began their meal, a dish of roasted peanuts was placed on the table as an appetiser. The men all helped themselves to the nuts. But, within a few moments, the unfortunate gentleman began to gag and complain he could not breathe. His tongue swelled and his lips took on a blue tinge. There was panic in the restaurant. Someone had the sense to call a doctor, but it was all too late. He died at the table, unable to breathe. My colleague at first could not explain the death, so he visited the restaurant to talk to the proprietors. They told him the men had only eaten peanuts. It was the head chef who provided the clue; he had heard of people being allergic to peanuts. In places where such nuts are commonly eaten I suppose the condition would crop up more frequently.

"My colleague continued his research at the various medical colleges and libraries in London. He finally unearthed a paper concerning a rare allergy to peanuts. He gave me the bare bones of the paper over the telephone. Some people, for an unexplained reason, suffer a fatal restriction of the airways when they consume peanuts. It is so uncommon that hardly anyone knows of the condition, but it is something that can run in families. Shortly after I learned about this, the Inspector rang and informed me that the vial contained peanut oil."

"Peanuts killed Zachary, Isaac and Annabel Graves?" Clara said.

"Their symptoms suggest it, though I don't know of a test to find traces of peanut oil in a dead person."

"But the rarity of peanut oil alone makes it curious that a vial should turn up in the Graves' household," Clara was starting to see the puzzle pieces coming together. "And it was discreetly hidden, as if someone knew it was dangerous."

"You don't go about hiding a harmless cooking oil for no reason," Park-Coombs helped himself to another scone. "Unless you know it is a little less than harmless to some of your family."

"Annabel knew," Clara muttered to herself. "She knew her brother was allergic to peanuts, probably knew about her father too. That was why she suspected she had been murdered."

"And yet, it also makes you wonder if she could have

been the murderer," Park-Coombs added.

"Is there any way of tracing where that vial came from?" Clara asked.

The Inspector scratched his moustache and gave the matter some thought.

"How many shops in London stock the stuff, that is my first question," he mused. "Then how many have sent any to Brighton, assuming the perpetrator of these crimes did not collect it from London in person."

"You must find out, Inspector. This is our first true lead on the murderer."

"But, why?" Annie asked. "Why kill three people? And in such a peculiar fashion."

"Motives are complex, Miss Green," the Inspector told her gently. "I think anyone who commits a murder is generally less than rational. I've seen people killed over such mundane things as a ruined rug or a smashed mirror."

"I think I may have a lead," Clara added. "Miss Rose Hart was most forthcoming, thank you for sending her to me Inspector."

Park-Coombs looked a little abashed.

"She is trying to build a better life for herself."

"I have a hunch, Inspector. I think Rose Hart is the daughter of Julia Graves and the very reason Julia was sent by her father to the Ladies' House of Reform."

The Inspector cocked his head.

"What does that mean to this case?"

"Perhaps nothing, perhaps everything. It certainly is a motive for Zachary Graves' murder. Revenge is always bitterest when it is between family members. But to confirm my suspicions I would need access to the files at the House of Reform, and I doubt they will just hand them over."

"You want a police inspector to give them a nudge," Park-Coombs' understood at once.

"Precisely, then it will be time to confront the Graves' family once more. It is plain now one of them is a murderer. Perhaps Annabel discovered who."

"The evidence of the forged will still points firmly to Julia," Park-Coombs reminded them all.

"Is she that stupid?" Clara asked herself. "Or rather, is she that desperate?"

She waited for an answer, but no one spoke. Everyone knew there was only one person who could answer that conundrum.

Chapter Twenty-two

It was now over a week since the unfortunate Mr Graves had been laid to rest in the cold Brighton soil. The newspapers were bored with the unsubstantiated rumours that he might have been murdered. They had turned their attention to a spate of forged train tickets circulating in Hove, and the growing danger pedestrians faced from the rising number of motorcars. Mr Graves was all but forgotten. Clara read her morning paper with her usual feeling of mild despair. How fickle the world was. How soon the news of yesterday became stale.

She put down the paper and glanced at Bramble.

"I am tired of being indoors," she informed the dog.

She collected her walking stick and hobbled into the front hall. She was just putting on her coat when the doorbell rang. Clara limped to the door and opened it. She was deeply surprised to see Isaac Graves' mother outside.

"May I come in? Or were you just going out?" Mrs Graves asked.

"Of course you may come in. I was only going to take a bit of fresh air, but that can wait until later," Clara escorted Mrs Graves into the parlour, which had rather become her interview room of late. "Can I get you anything?"

"Please don't bother. I see you take the Brighton Gazette?"

Clara nodded.

"I had asked them to run a piece dispelling all these silly rumours about my son being murdered," Mrs Graves gave a sigh. "They didn't. I suppose it is academic now anyway. At least they have not learned about poor Annabel yet."

Clara lowered herself into a chair slowly, wondering what to say. Did Mrs Graves know that her daughter had been murdered?

"The Inspector called on me late yesterday evening," Mrs Graves explained to spare her the confusion. "He told me that my daughter had whispered she was murdered before she died and that someone had searched my home while we were at the hospital and found a vial of peanut oil. I found that very underhand of the police, I might add, but I am really not in a position to complain. This casts a whole new light on Isaac's death."

"Isaac was allergic to peanuts, then?"

"Yes. As was my late husband."

"May I ask, how did you discover they had such an allergy?"

Mrs Graves gave a gentle shrug of her shoulders.

"It was one of those awful chance events, Miss Fitzgerald, one I shall never forget. It was in the 1880s, when the children were still small. Zachary had worked himself into the ground that summer. He was utterly exhausted and the doctor prescribed a complete break from all work for six months. As the winter was drawing in, we decided to go abroad. America took our fancy, there are some regions there that have very mild winters. We agreed we would tour the country and visit all the fine cities," Mrs Graves shook her head. "While we were there we attended a rodeo, a very strange experience. They attempt to ride unbroken horses, or even cattle. I could not quite see the appeal, but there were real cowboys and that fascinated the children. In any case, we were at this rodeo for several hours and there were men and women going about selling all manner of food. We had tried 'hot dogs' and 'corn on the cob', all very novel. Then someone sold us a bag of these little nuts. Zachary tried one first. He declared they were mild, but pleasant and offered the bag to the children. They had only just picked out a handful each when Zachary began to gag and gasp. It was the most frightening experience of my life, Miss Fitzgerald! He clutched at his throat and could not catch his breath.

"We caused quite the scene! Thankfully, one of the rodeo patrons was a country doctor who had seen just such a case once before. He found a quiet place for my husband to rest and insisted he drink water to try and flush his system. In the panic I hardly thought of the handful of nuts each child had taken. They had dropped them in the confusion, but then Isaac began to splutter too, followed by Christiana. Before I knew it all my dears, aside from little Julia, were gagging and gasping like their father.

"The doctor had them all sit still and explained to me that it was the peanuts. Some people reacted badly to them. However, when questioned, the children assured me they had not eaten any of the nuts after seeing their father so ill. The doctor informed me that some people only need smell a peanut to react to it! The children had handled the nuts and then touched their faces. Fortunately, because of this limited contact, they recovered quite rapidly. Their father took longer. He was ill for several days and we thought we would lose him."

"It must have been an awful experience," Clara sympathised.

"It was. Which is why when the Inspector said…" Mrs Graves had to stop to gulp back tears. "Miss Fitzgerald, I am not a woman who shows her emotions. It was how I was raised. Some perceive me as cold for that, I am not. When I learned that Annabel had been poisoned with peanut oil I knew at once that someone in my immediate family must have committed the awful crime, and my heart broke. No one outside of our family circle was ever told of the affliction. My husband was a very private man and preferred to put the incident behind him. One of my daughters must, therefore, be a killer."

Clara looked at Mrs Graves steadily.

"You have discounted one person in this matter."

Mrs Graves started.

"Who?"

"Yourself, Mrs Graves. You too knew of the condition."

"But I killed no one!" Mrs Graves was stunned. "How could you say such a thing?"

"Is it so harsh considering you have already declared one of your daughters guilty of murder? After all, I only have your word for your innocence."

Mrs Graves fell silent. She pulled at her fingers unconsciously, giving each finger a tug in turn with the opposite hand.

"You have a point, but I didn't do it."

"There have been three unexplained deaths in your family, Mrs Graves. I believe all of them link to the same person or persons. But I am lacking a motive."

"Do not look at me, please. Since that day all those years ago I have avoided nuts of any description. To know there was a vial of peanut oil in my house turns my stomach. It takes so little to trigger a reaction in an affected person, and each time the person is exposed the reaction is greater. The doctor explained all this to my husband when he recovered. He made it very plain that he must avoid even touching a peanut at all costs. He stated that he feared a second incident would finish my husband off."

"Did the children know this?"

"Oh yes, well we had to protect them! You do not really see peanuts in this country, but who is to say we won't start importing them in the future? I have seen bags of them being sold at circuses, after all. The children had to be warned."

Clara understood, but it opened up her field of suspects a little too wide.

"Why would any of your daughters wish their father, brother and sister dead, Mrs Graves?"

"I couldn't say," Mrs Graves wiped a tear from her eye. "It is an evil thing to do."

"I have heard stories that your husband was difficult to live with," Clara pressed, hoping Mrs Graves would give her something.

"He was strict, but only for the children's own good. He had seen too many cases of men taking advantage of young ladies with money. He would not have that happen to his girls."

"So he prevented them having suitors?"

"You make it sound so harsh! He merely kept a close watch. He preferred the girls not to go out to dances and such, yes, but only because he worried about them."

"Was he strict with the household finances too?"

Mrs Graves looked uncomfortable. She had not been aware of how much Clara had heard about her late husband.

"We never had quite the amount of money people imagined. To keep a fine roof over our heads my husband had to work all the hours God sent. There was very little left over for luxuries. I admit, Zachary was rather prone to spending what little spare we had on the servants. He felt sorry for them and imagined they would benefit more from having money spent on them than the girls who, after all, lived very comfortably."

"But such actions might have created resentment?"

"Perhaps. But he was not unkind."

"What of Julia?" Clara countered. "What of her being sent to the House of Reform? That was hardly an act of kindness."

Mrs Graves had gone pale. She moved her mouth as if wanting to speak, but was silent. Finally she concluded she must say something.

"Julia was always a wild child. She found herself in trouble. Heaven knows how!" Mrs Graves looked deeply sad. "I blame myself. I never devoted the time to her I did to the others. She was the youngest and I always seemed so busy. Julia was left to her own devices. She was always fighting with her father too. They never saw eye-to-eye."

"It is curious she was the only one not to inherit her father's condition."

Mrs Graves reddened. Clara spotted the reaction and knew she had hit upon a nerve. But what could it be?

"Who was the father of Julia's child, Mrs Graves?"

"I don't know. She never told me nor her father. That was why he became so angry and sent her away. If only she had told him. Perhaps we could have arranged a marriage, made everything good again. But she kept silent and her father became infuriated. My poor Zachary believed that reputation was everything in his line of work and he could not afford the scandal. Julia was sent away secretly to have the baby. The Ladies' House of Reform seemed as good a place as any. They were discreet and no one there would know who Julia was. I admit it upset me and Julia. She never forgave us for making her give up the child."

"Did she hate her father?"

"No!" Mrs Graves almost threw up her hands in horror. "How could she?"

"Then who had the motive to kill Zachary?"

Mrs Graves shook her head.

"I don't know. I don't know. None of my girls are killers..." she finally burst into tears. "Only that isn't true, is it? One of my girls killed them all. How could this have happened?"

Clara could not offer her an answer. She reached out for Mrs Graves' hand and attempted to comfort her.

"I fear that the police believe Julia the most likely suspect," she said when the woman had composed herself a little. "Because of the will forged in her favour."

"Oh, but that is nonsense!"

"Is it, Mrs Graves? Who but Julia benefited from that will?"

Mrs Graves began to cry again, her old shoulders hunched and she sobbed as if her heart was breaking afresh. For a long time there was nothing Clara could do but hold her hand. When the tears had finally run their course, Mrs Graves managed to speak.

"Julia did not forge that will."

Her tone was so adamant that Clara was surprised.

"If not her, then who? No one else benefited from the new will. Her sisters can hardly be blamed."

"Your handwriting expert is wrong. Isaac must have written it!"

Clara watched Mrs Graves' face as she spoke. She could not meet Clara's eyes, she looked instead to the fireplace.

"Isaac Graves did not write that will. He would not have isolated his other sisters, nor his mother. If Julia did not write the document herself, then the person who did was someone who wanted to make amends. Someone with a guilty conscience."

Clara held Mrs Graves' hands firmly.

"Mrs Graves, if you have anything you wish to confess…"

"Me!" Mrs Graves blinked, but her shocked expression was unconvincing.

"The will gives Julia the motive to kill her brother. It puts the noose around her neck. Unless someone else comes forward and confesses to writing it."

Mrs Graves' eyes darted about furiously.

"Whatever can you mean?" she began, then she licked her lips and hesitated. "Poor Julia, always taking the blame for other people's sins."

"She didn't write the will then?"

Another long pause.

"No."

"Did you, Mrs Graves?"

The clock chimed the quarter hour while Mrs Graves

sat in silence thinking about what she must say. At last she seemed to rouse herself.

"I wrote that will," she admitted.

"Why?"

Mrs Graves gave a soft laugh, as if the confession had eased her heart a little.

"Julia deserves so much more, Miss Fitzgerald. But she is always the forgotten daughter, the one last remembered. That is as much my fault as anyone else's, perhaps more so. I wanted to give her something. I wanted her for once to have enough money to have everything she desired."

"Which is why you forged the will?"

"Yes."

"You wrote out yourself and your other daughters, not to mention Isaac Graves' wife, just to ease your guilt over neglecting Julia? I don't believe you, Mrs Graves."

"Nor should you," Mrs Graves' agreed. "For I have only told you a fraction of the truth. There is a very good reason Julia did not inherit her father's condition."

"Zachary was not her father?" Clara guessed.

"No. And he knew that too. I sometimes think that was why he was so hard on her. You were right, Miss Fitzgerald, I forged that will out of guilt. Guilt that an innocent child paid for my sin of adultery. I always felt he sent her away because she was not his…" Mrs Graves' shuddered. "I saw no other way to make amends but to alter Isaac's will so she could have all his money. At least that would be something. She would no longer be the left out child."

"What of your other daughters?"

"My husband's investments would have seen us comfortable. I admit, I was cruel to Isaac's wife. I wasn't thinking when I wrote the will. I have always been a good mimic of others' handwriting, and I knew Isaac's hand very well. In any case, I always thought he would outlive me, and I had a few shares and other stocks tucked away that the other girls could have."

"How did you get the old will out of the safe at Isaac's office?"

"Oh, I have known the combination for his safe for years. When he was ill he asked me to bring him some documents from it. Do you know, it was only one number different from the combination of my late husband's own safe," Mrs Graves shook her head. "But only I knew the combination, he told no one else. I swear."

"Would you be prepared to state this to the police?"

"To spare Julia it is the least I can do."

"You realise you have given yourself a motive for murder? Perhaps you feared Isaac would find you out?"

Mrs Graves gave a long sigh.

"I didn't kill my son. But I shall not let someone else pay the price for my crimes yet again. I have been foolish, and now I must face the consequences."

"I believe you, Mrs Graves."

"Good," Mrs Graves looked solemn. "Then I ask one last thing. Find the murderer among my children."

Chapter Twenty-three

Mrs Graves entreaty stayed in Clara's thoughts, nagging at her, cajoling her, pleading to her. The problem was there was no real evidence to show who the murderer was. Annabel's death was clearly intentional, but clues to precisely who committed the crime were absent. With Mrs Graves' admitting she had forged the will, the one scrape of evidence against Julia was gone. Clara knew there was only one way they were going to catch the person responsible for three murders – the killer would have to be persuaded to confess.

Clara informed the Inspector of her visit from Mrs Graves and her own thoughts on the case. They agreed between them that the only course of action was to confront the remaining Graves women and endeavour to rattle the killer enough to make a mistake. It was a long shot, and they would only get one chance. If they failed to get their confession, then a murderer would walk free.

They arrived at the Graves' house a little after one o'clock. The Inspector had borrowed the one and only car within in the Brighton police force to carry Clara there in relative comfort. She was not to be omitted from this final showdown.

Glynis the maid met them on the doorstep.

"I called ahead," the Inspector told her.

"Yes sir," Glynis nodded. "They are all in the morning room. Shall I show you?"

"Just before you do that," Clara stopped Glynis. "I have one question for you…"

A few moments later Clara and the Inspector were sitting in the morning room at the breakfast table. Facing them were Julia, Agatha, Mrs Graves and Christiana. The girls looked worried. Mrs Graves looked old and sad. Her hands trembled.

"Thank you for allowing us to call," Clara began politely. "This has been a truly awful business and I know you must all be deeply in shock."

"Annabel was murdered, then," Christiana spoke stiffly. "That's why you are here. Isaac too. Someone murdered them both."

"Yes," Clara said gently. "But this case is complicated by the manner of death of the victims, which was quite unusual and very specific to your family. Isaac and Annabel both died from a fatal reaction to peanut oil."

Clara watched for reactions. She noted that Julia jumped, Agatha seemed to accept the news stoically and Christiana was very close to tears.

"Let me lay the facts of the case before you all again. Isaac Graves died suddenly. Upon his desk was a glass of water, which we have been told over and over was completely out of character. He hated water near his work. To add to the confusion, Mr Erikson insists he heard someone enter Mr Graves' office after his last client had left. But who was that visitor? Next we have the mystery of some missing legal documents that had been on Isaac's desk. Were these stolen on purpose or by accident, the killer thinking they were something else? We know who these papers concerned and that person was blackmailed into handing over money for them. They thought they recognised the voice of the person behind the blackmail. But, these rather random clues only tell us Mr Graves' death was suspicious, not who killed him,"

Clara paused for dramatic effect, watching the faces of her audience closely. Still there was no indication of a guilty conscience among them. "Next we have the matter of Isaac's last will. The peculiarity of him leaving all his money to one sister caught our attention. We now know that the will was forged and, at first, that seemed the clue we needed to trace the murderer. However, we now know who was behind the will and it seems they are not our suspect."

"Who forged the will?" Agatha asked, her eyes flitting to Julia. "That is a crime, is it not? They must be punished."

"They tried to cheat us of our inheritance," Christiana joined the debate, her eyes also went to Julia. "They should be ashamed of themselves."

"How can we be sure they did not kill Isaac and Annabel?" Agatha added. "I think you should arrest this person, Inspector!"

"Then you must see your mother go to prison," Mrs Graves was sitting very upright as she interrupted the argument. "For I forged the will."

"Mother!" Christiana spluttered. "Why would you do such a thing?"

"You left us with nothing in favour of Julia!" Agatha snapped.

"Nonsense. Your father's investments would have kept you comfortable and you inherit from my own will. I never imagined I would outlive your brother."

"But... why?" the voice that spoke up was Julia's, she was looking as surprised as the others, but her tone was soft.

Mrs Graves had to compose herself before she could speak. She reached for a handkerchief.

"I wanted you to have something, Julia. I wanted to make amends. My own money is tied up in stocks and shares, but Isaac had a small fortune and I thought..." Mrs Graves' dabbed at her eyes. "You always wanted a little cottage by the sea and a pretty garden. You wanted peace and quiet. I was never able to give you that, but with Isaac's fortune you could have it. I meant to discuss the matter with him, but then he became so gravely ill and I panicked. If he died before we could make the arrangements his fortune would be divided. So I created a new will and substituted it for the old one. Isaac never knew. For a man so careful with other people's wills, he never thought about his own. When he recovered, the urgency was gone, but I never seemed to find the time or the courage to broach the subject with him again."

"You cut us out of his will for Julia?" Christiana was aghast. "What have we done to you to deserve such treatment?"

"You would have been comfortable," Mrs Graves assured her. "There would have been a roof over your heads."

"Yes, in some rundown terrace among shopkeepers and labourers while Julia was in her cottage!" Christiana snarled.

"It would not have been like that. I was too hasty with the will, I made it too one-sided. I regret deeply forgetting poor Isaac's wife, but she is so easy to forget."

"You still have not explained why?" Agatha said in anguish. "Have we offended you somehow?"

Mrs Graves was too emotional to speak. Clara intervened.

"Guilt sometimes makes us do irrational things," she said. "A guilty conscience can cause us to commit crimes we otherwise would never dream of."

"Guilt?" Christiana was looking utterly baffled. "Guilt at what? Julia, what is this all about?"

"I don't know," Julia replied.

"Did you put mother up to this? What hold have you over her?"

"I have no hold!"

"Girls!" Mrs Graves spread out her hands and waved them into silence. "Julia has no more knowledge of this matter than you do. Yet, once again, she is the one paying the price for my sins."

"What sins?" Christiana demanded.

"I shall explain, only because I want this matter resolved and for Julia to be absolved of all blame. She had nothing to do with the will. I altered it because I wanted to make amends. All these years, Julia, I have borne a burden of guilt, knowing how your father treated you. How he sent you away. All because of what I had done," Mrs Graves took a shaky breath. "I faltered in my marriage vows. Zachary worked such long hours and was too tired when he came home to have time for me. I grew lonely and I found comfort elsewhere."

Everyone was sitting in stunned silence. Julia's eyes were wide as she realised what her mother was saying.

"Zachary always knew he was not Julia's father. I could not hide it. For that reason he was always cold to her and sterner towards her than the others. Somehow, that infected the other girls' feelings towards her too. She was always the outsider. Only Isaac treated her lovingly. I have felt responsible for that alienation all these years, and then I had an idea how I could make amends…" Mrs Graves began to sob. "But I did not kill Isaac or Annabel. How could I?"

"No, you are not responsible for their deaths," Clara agreed. "But their murderer is sat at this table."

Christiana and Agatha both looked appalled and fit to walk from the room. They were still reeling from the news their mother had cut them from Isaac's will because she was an adulteress. They looked as though any more of this shock news might finish them off. Julia, on the other hand, was silent and looking firmly at the table.

"The problem all along with this case has been a lack of motive," Clara continued. "None of you seemed to have a reason to kill Isaac. I suspected it all came down to family secrets. As for Annabel, well, I still don't know why you decided to poison her, Julia."

Clara looked directly at Julia who met her gaze with a strange, steely look.

"Julia?" Agatha gulped.

"You took the water jug into your sister's bedroom the night before she died," Clara continued. "Glynis told me you were most considerate that night, noting how tired she looked and insisting on taking Annabel's water jug. Did you lace the jug or her glass with the peanut oil?"

"You have no proof," Julia responded.

"I admit it is very circumstantial. But juries have convicted people on far less. Besides, there is the other matter."

"Other matter?" Mrs Graves was looking flustered. She had thought she had just spared her youngest daughter from arrest, now it seemed Julia was in far more trouble than just that caused by an act of forgery.

"I think perhaps it is time we talked alone, Julia," Clara said.

The Inspector rose from the table and very politely ushered Julia's sisters out the door. They looked rather relieved to be escaping. Mrs Graves was more truculent.

"I shall remain with Julia!" she insisted.

"Go, mother," her daughter responded. "I don't need you here."

Mrs Graves looked heartbroken.

"But Julia…"

"Go! I don't want you to be here. You will no doubt hear all about it later, but by then so will all of Brighton."

Mrs Graves looked sick. She stumbled from the table and had to take the Inspector's arm to make it out of the door. She paused one last time to look at her daughter, then disappeared. The Inspector closed the door to the morning room behind her.

"How much do you know?" Julia asked Clara, now they were alone.

"Enough," Clara lied, she couldn't allow Julia to know that without a confession they had nothing. "We know about Rose Hart."

Julia gave a sad nod.

"Poor Rose. It was meant to be so different…" she

started to cry.

"Rose is your daughter. Isaac spotted her and recognised her at once. She looked just like you."

"I was devastated to know she had ended up in that place," Julia sobbed. "They promised me she would have a good life, in a loving family. They lied!"

"This morning the Inspector and I went to look at the records on Rose Hart. They were very thorough and included her medical history. Apparently, that is a requirement of going into the place. We were most curious to see that Rose had been hospitalised once with breathing problems. She had been at the fair, walking with a man who was eating peanuts," Clara let this news sink in. "A peanut allergy is an extremely rare condition that can run in families, or so I am told. Your father had the condition and passed it to all his children. Only, you are not his child. So how could Rose have it? A strange coincidence? Neither myself, nor the Inspector, believe in those. Rather, we believe she inherited the condition from her father. Was Zachary Graves Rose's father?"

Julia almost laughed.

"No," she said. "My father had little love for me, but he was not that sort of man."

"Then…" Clara paused, what she was about to suggest seemed almost impossible, though she knew it was not. "Then, Isaac...?"

"Why do you think I could not tell my father?" Julia had a strange smile on her face. "Isaac and I, we were always close. I was so lost when he went away to school, and then he came back. He had grown so very handsome. We had only ever had time for each other. We knew what we did was wrong, but we didn't care. I still do not. I loved Isaac. He married to please my father, but I always knew he only ever loved me."

"For the love of…" the Inspector rubbed a hand over his face. He had seen some things in his time, but he was still thrown by cases of incest.

"Then, why did you kill him?" Clara pressed on, trying

not to think too hard about what they had just learned.

"I didn't!" Julia snapped. "I loved him!"

"But, you killed Annabel?"

Julia's lips curled into a snarl.

"Annabel," she said bitterly. "I wish I had not done so. Then I would have the satisfaction of seeing her swing!"

"Then she killed Isaac?" Clara was astounded.

"It might as well have been murder. She forced Isaac to commit suicide. You were right about the glass. He drank water laced with peanut oil in front of Annabel."

"She had learned about Rose?"

"No, that is the irony of it! She never knew about Isaac and I," Julia gave a bitter laugh. "What does it matter now, anyway? Annabel was always our father's favourite. She was his oldest daughter. She never accepted that his death was an accident and she kept poking and prodding the matter, never letting it be. Over the years we grew quite bored with her. And then, at long last, she found something. She discovered that Isaac had not been away in London at a lunch meeting as he had always said when father died. She found out he had lied. The person he was supposed to be meeting was this professor of law. But the professor had just published some papers and in one of them he mentioned that he had spent six months in 1899 abroad. Isaac could not have met him and Annabel realised this.

"Perhaps she had always suspected my brother. Perhaps this was just the last piece of the puzzle. But she was convinced by the uncovering of this false alibi that Isaac had been in Brighton the day my father died and that he had killed him."

"Isaac Graves murdered his father?" the Inspector mumbled.

"In revenge for father sending me away and forcing me to give up Rose!" Julia exploded. "He did it for me! I never knew until later. He ordered the peanut oil from London."

"And Annabel worked this out?" asked Clara.

"Somehow," Julia nodded. "I never got around to asking her how before I dealt with her."

Julia suddenly had a sinister smile on her face.

"It always seemed odd the way Isaac died like my father. But, I was prepared to think it natural until people starting asking questions. I knew it had to be one of us who had killed him. His death was so like father's, it must have been from peanut oil, and only the family knew about that. Even Glynis doesn't know," Julia stretched out her hands on the table before her. "In truth, I don't much mind being found out. At least now people will know what Annabel did."

"They will also learn what you did," the Inspector said bluntly. "And what your brother did."

"So be it!" Julia snapped. "My brother and I did nothing wrong. We were in love. My father deserved to die after how he treated me. And Annabel was the same. She should never have harmed Isaac!"

"How did you find out it was Annabel?" Clara asked quietly, trying to defuse some of the anger stirring up in Julia. For the first time she was beginning to understand why her family had called her 'wild'. There was something a tad insane about her manner.

"She was such a fool! It wasn't hard to discover her," Julia gave a sniff of derision. "When I realised what must have happened I kept my eyes open for clues among the family as to who had been behind Isaac's murder. By chance, I went to Annabel's room looking for some hand cream. She keeps a pot in a drawer in her dressing table. I opened it and there was this glass vial. It looked odd so I picked it up, took out the stopper and smelt it. It had the faintest of odours, something familiar. So I put some on my finger and tried it. Yes, it was peanut oil! I remembered the taste from all those years past when Isaac bought some. He let me try it, because I was the only one in the family who was not allergic, and he wanted to know if it would be tasted in water. I knew at once the only reason Annabel had that bottle was so she could kill Isaac.

"I hid the vial in Isaac's room. It seemed fittingly ironic. Then I confronted Annabel. I told her I knew what she had done, but I needed to know why? That was when she told me she had learned that Isaac had killed father and in a moment of fury she had bought the peanut oil and plotted his death. She slipped into his offices when all was quiet and confronted him. There was no argument. She just told him what she knew and that, if he did not drink the peanut oil and kill himself, she would go to the police and the papers. Even if it could not be proved, a shadow would be cast over his reputation. For Isaac, like my father, reputation meant everything. I suppose he was also afraid that our secret would be discovered. In the end, he agreed to Annabel's demands. He would die just like our father did. A fitting revenge, in Annabel's eyes, and not murder, or so she said, because Isaac took the oil and laced his own glass of water. Then she watched him die."

"Did she tell you why she stole the Hatton divorce papers from his desk?" Clara asked.

"Papers? No. Though Annabel was always looking for ways to get extra money. She regularly booked charabanc tours with Mr Hatton, you know."

Clara sat back in her chair. She had wanted a confession, but somehow the cold calculating way the Graves family had dealt with its private problems was a little more than she wanted to know. The Inspector interceded.

"How did you kill Annabel?"

"It was simple really. I made her trust me. After she confessed, and, oh, she confessed easily! After she confessed, she asked me what I would do. I told her I intended to do nothing, because I had already lost too many members of my family. I said I had thrown away the peanut oil, so there was no evidence of her actions. I would not go to the police, I promised, but I would always know what she had done. She believed me! She was actually grateful for my understanding!" Julia shook her head with a sneer. "She made me sick. So desperate and gullible. I walked away knowing I would kill her. That night I put a small drop of peanut oil in her drinking glass and then I waited. It takes very little of the oil to create a fatal reaction in our family. Had it not worked the first night, I would have put more in the following night. I would have killed her eventually."

Julia held their gazes.

"I'm not sorry. She killed Isaac."

A heavy silence fell over them. The shock of this revelation took a moment to sink in. Then slowly Inspector Park-Coombs rose.

"Miss Graves, I will have to arrest you now," he said.

Julia tilted her head and flared her nose.

"I thought I was cleverer than Annabel. I see now I was wrong. Oh well, it is not as though I have a great deal to live for, what with Isaac gone. Mother thought money would make me happy. You see how this family thinks? Only Isaac understood me," Julia rose from the table. "May I request that my daughter's name be kept from those awful newsmen? She has suffered enough. It is the least I can do."

"I won't release her name," Park-Coombs agreed. "And I think her files at the Ladies' House of Reform might just happen to get lost in my office safe. Just in case."

"Thank you Inspector."

Julia went quietly. In the hallway of the house Mrs Graves stood trembling, her two surviving daughters watching on as Julia was led away. There was nothing to be said. Mrs Graves had wanted the murderer among her children found. She had ended up finding three.

Chapter Twenty-four

The papers were quick enough to latch hold of the story of Julia's arrest. They reported every piece of scandal they could find. Julia assisted by given interviews from her prison cell as she awaited her trial. Despite her lawyer endeavouring to convince her to say nothing, Julia was loath to miss giving her side of the story. Soon the whole sordid saga was being published in black and white – her time at the House of Reform, Isaac's revenge on his father, Annabel's revenge on Isaac. The only part Julia neatly avoided was revealing her relationship with her brother. It was unlikely it would ever be revealed, as it was not necessary to the case. Annabel had not killed Isaac because she knew of his incestuous affair with his sister, and Isaac's dabbles with murder could be explained as the actions of a loving brother incensed by his father's cruelty towards his sister. Their secret need never be revealed. Which was just as well, as the Inspector preferred not to think of the harm it might do to poor Rose Hart, the true victim in this case of familial depravity. She need never know of her true origins; though Clara suspected she was intelligent enough to make the connection between her strange illness and Isaac's sudden interest in her background. Hopefully she would only realise that Julia was her mother, and her father's identity would remain secret.

Clara was rather glad the case was over. It had not only been challenging, but rather unpleasant. Murder always was, but especially when it so ripped apart a family. She would never be able to go past the solicitors' office again without thinking of Isaac and his sister, and feeling a pang of nausea in her belly. Miss Parker had been right when she said there was something wrong about Isaac Graves.

Fortunately, life had a habit of getting in the way of such disturbing thoughts. Tommy had his appointment with Dr Cutt for a start. Clara put down the newspaper from which she had been reading the latest Julia Graves interview and hobbled to the dining room to see how things were going.

Dr Cutt had hypnotised Tommy and had him out of his wheelchair and walking about the room. Clara watched from the doorway, all thoughts of the strange Graves family cast from her mind. Annie came up beside her.

"He walks well. Just a slight limp," she nodded. "Did you see the latest report on our case in the papers?"

Clara had to smile at the reference to 'our case'. She didn't imagine she would be able to persuade Annie to ever play detective again, but it was good to see she had taken this case to heart.

"Yes, they printed the latest interview," Clara said in a hushed tone.

"It's ghastly to think what people get up to in private," Annie tutted. "To think I felt sorry for Miss Julia and gave her the benefit of the doubt."

"I think we all did," Clara went quiet as Dr Cutt approached Tommy.

"Now, Tommy," he said in his calm, gentle tone. "I want you to remain standing right where you are and, when I count down from three to one, you will wake up. You will stir from this place of calm you are in and you will open your eyes and, when you do, you will see you are standing upright and you will be of the firm and certain belief that you can walk. Are you ready? Now, 3... 2... 1..."

Tommy opened his eyes and looked at Dr Cutt. For a second he just smiled at him and gave a yawn, then he swayed a little, and suddenly Tommy realised he was standing upright and was not in his chair. He looked down at his legs and the shock of being firmly on his own two feet almost made him tumble backwards in surprise. Dr Cutt quickly grabbed his arm.

"I do believe you can walk, Mr Fitzgerald," the good doctor put his arm through Tommy's and, a little stiffly, escorted him about the room in a slow walk.

After a few moments Tommy's strength seemed to give out and the doctor helped him into his chair. He smiled at his patient. Tommy was still staring at his legs and blinking back tears of joy.

"Good God!" he said, wiping at an eye discreetly. "I never thought I would walk again. I feel quite an idiot keeping myself stuck in this chair all these years when my legs were in perfect order."

"Oh nonsense!" Clara came over and hugged her brother. "You do speak some codswallop!"

"Old girl, I can walk!" Tommy said with a slight sniff. "I can bloody walk!"

At that moment Bramble bustled into the room with a slipper in his mouth and jumped onto Tommy's lap.

"Ah, I didn't know you had a poodle!" Dr Cutt leaned forward and gave the dog a rub behind the ears.

"He is not ours," Clara explained. "We found him and have been trying to find his owners ever since. He needs a good home."

"Well," Dr Cutt smiled at Bramble. "It so happens I have a delightful patient who is deeply fond of poodles. I have no doubt she would take on this little chap in an instant."

"Really?" Clara said, looking at Bramble with a

twinkle in her eye. "He does rather eat shoes."

"I don't think she minds that," Dr Cutt promised. "I could take him to her now, if you would like. I shall be seeing her in half an hour to discuss her tennis elbow."

"That would be most helpful," Clara agreed. "He is not a bad chap, but we are not really a household suited to dogs. What do you say, Tommy?"

Tommy had gone very quiet; the joy of the discovery he could walk had evaporated. He looked at Bramble sadly.

"I suppose so," he said softly. "He does rather raid the larder."

He gave Bramble a gentle squeeze.

"And he has a nightmarish habit of tearing up socks," Tommy stared at the little dog, which looked back at him with appealing brown eyes. "She would look after him, would she?"

"She is a very kind and caring person. Her dogs come first in all things," Dr Cutt assured him.

Tommy gave a small sigh.

"Well Bramble, its time you trotted along, old boy."

"Oh, for crying out loud!" Annie strolled into the room. "The pair of you make me despair!"

She stood with her hands on her hips looking at Tommy and Clara as if they were a pair of very silly children.

"Dr Cutt that dog is going nowhere," she said stoutly. "Tommy needs to walk daily to get those legs working properly, and I know of no better way for getting a person to walk than by giving them a dog."

"That is very true," Dr Cutt agreed amiably.

"But, Bramble drives you up the wall," Tommy said to Annie. "He steals food and pulls the washing off the line and…"

"And you think the world of him," Annie interrupted. "I ain't so hard as to see a man who has been through a war go broken-hearted over a dog. Bramble stays. Besides, I just bought this."

Annie rummaged in her apron pocket and produced a smart leather lead and collar. On the collar was a shiny tag engraved with the name 'Bramble'. She handed it to Tommy, and he looked rather choked again.

"Well, I do believe everything has worked out for the best," Dr Cutt smiled. "I shall call again next week, young man, and I expect to see you walking."

Tommy could hardly speak to promise he would be. Clara propped herself against the table and looked at their new addition. Bramble gave her a hard stare, as if he knew she had just tried to get rid of him. Then he jumped from Tommy's lap and leapt up at her legs. She was clearly forgiven.

Dr Cutt was just showing himself out as the phone rang and Annie answered it. Clara, still in the dining room, smiled at her brother.

"You should have said you wanted to keep the dog."

Tommy gave her a shrug.

"I thought you and Annie disliked him."

Annie reappeared in the room. She was smiling.

"That was Mr Hatton on the telephone. Apparently he is so pleased at the way you handled his problem discreetly that he wants to thank you. It seems all this pickle over his missing papers actually got him and his wife talking," Annie rolled her eyes. "Really, some people make life so complicated."

"So he rang to say thank you?" Clara confirmed.

"Oh, not just that. No. He was so delighted that he has arranged tickets for us to all go on a charabanc tour of the Lake District," Annie grinned. "Doesn't that sound delightful?"

Clara glanced sourly at her sore foot.

"Well, at least I won't have to walk," she sighed.

"Just one question," Tommy looked up at them both. "Do they allow dogs?"

Printed in Great Britain
by Amazon

75777977R00128